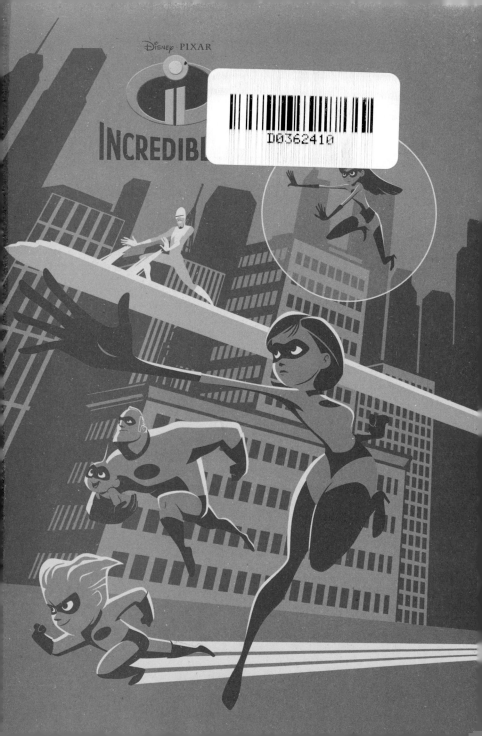

Published in the United States by Random House Children's Books, a division
of Penguin Random House LLC, 1745 Broadway, New York, NY 10019,
and in Canada by Penguin Random House Canada Limited, Toronto.
Random House and the colophon are registered trademarks of Penguin
Random House LLC.

rhcbooks.com

ISBN 978-0-7364-3851-3 (hardcover)
ISBN 978-0-7364-3850-6 (paperback)

Printed in the United States of America

10 9 8 7 6 5 4 3

INCREDIBLES 2

The Junior Novelization

Adapted by **Suzanne Francis**

Random House 🏠 New York

Prologue

Inside a windowless room, a stark white light flooded the darkness.

"File 82-712, Agent Rick Dicker interrogating," the straight-faced secret agent said into a microphone. His deep voice showed no emotion as he prepared to question the awkward-looking teenage boy sitting before him. "State your name, please."

The boy squirmed in his chair and winced, squinting at the blinding light. "Uh . . . ," he began. "Tony. Tony Rydinger."

"Tell me about the incident," Dicker said.

"Well, there was this girl. . . ." As Tony began to recount the story, he saw the memory play out in his mind. He remembered it clearly—walking up to a girl from his school during a track meet and talking to her.

"You're, uhh—Violet, right?" Tony had said.

"That's me," said Violet, smiling at him.

"You look . . . different," said Tony.

"I feel different," said Violet confidently.

Tony told Dicker he sort of knew her, but it seemed like she had changed.

"She was more sure of herself than before," he said. "Cool. Cute." He blushed a little, then quickly cleared his throat and continued to relay the story, explaining how he and Violet had made plans to see a movie together. Then they'd gone back to their seats to watch the track meet.

Everything had seemed normal until Tony and his friends were walking through the parking lot on their way home. The ground suddenly began to rumble and quake! The shaking became more and more violent—then an enormous armored vehicle with a powerful earthmover drill attached to the front exploded from the ground! It flipped cars out of its way, and Tony and his friends ran in different directions, trying to escape.

Tony squatted behind a car and peered around it to watch as chaos enveloped the city. Through the thicket of cars and panicked crowds, he saw a platform slowly extend from the vehicle, rising into the air. Then a hulking super villain appeared, standing on it. He was covered in armor, had clamplike metal hands, and wore an oversized mining helmet. His voice boomed across the city as he introduced himself with an evil cackle.

"Behold the Underminer!" he said. "I am always beneath you, but nothing is beneath *me*!"

Tony tried to stay hidden as the Underminer continued.

"I hereby declare war . . . on peace and happiness!"

Tony began searching for an escape route and scrambled behind another car. Then he noticed a strange pair of tall boots over red spandex.

"You two stay here," said a man's voice.

"Wait—should we be doing this? It is still illegal?" a woman said.

Tony told Dicker that at the time, he had thought the man and woman were Superheroes.

Tony listened as they continued to argue back and forth for a few moments. Then the Underminer disappeared into the tunneling vehicle, and it began to drill down into the earth.

"One of you patrol the perimeter, keep the crowds back and safe. The other watch Jack-Jack!" said the woman.

"But I thought we were gonna go with—" said a girl.

"You heard your mother!" said the man.

Tony recalled seeing the two adults taking off after the Underminer.

"I call perimeter!" said a boy.

"You're not going anywhere, you maggoty little creep!" said the girl.

Tony saw his chance to get out, but as he listened to the kids argue, he recognized the girl's voice.

"Oh, great," the girl said. "He gets to be a hero while I'm stuck ALONE in a parking lot, babysitting like an *idiot*!" She pulled off her mask and threw it to the ground. Tony stared at her, taking in the sight of the Supersuit. He told Dicker he knew she had sounded familiar. . . . It was Violet! He couldn't believe it.

Violet saw Tony. She tried to tell him everything was fine, but the situation was too weird for him to handle. So without knowing how to react, he just ran away.

In the interrogation room, Dicker switched on a strange machine that was mounted to the ceiling.

"I feel kinda bad about it," said Tony as Dicker pointed a laser beam between Tony's eyebrows. "Maybe I should've said hi or something? It's not her fault Superheroes are illegal. And it's not like I don't like strong girls. I'm pretty secure . . . manhood-wise. . . .

What is that?" Tony asked, finally noticing the strange gadget.

"Have you told anyone else about this?" asked Dicker, ignoring his question. "Your parents?"

"No," said Tony. "They'd only think I was hiding something. You know what I mean?"

"Sure, kid," said Dicker.

"I like this girl, Mr. Dicker," said Tony. "I'm supposed to go out with her Friday night. Now things are just gonna be . . . weird. I wish I could forget I ever saw her in that suit."

"You will, kid," said Dicker. "You will."

Just then, a small suction cup fired from the machine and stuck to Tony's forehead. His eyes fluttered for a moment, and everything went black.

1

Mr. Incredible clung to the top of the Underminer's massive tunneler as it chewed through the earth. He held on with all his strength, but the machine soon shook him loose, flinging him to the ground! He gagged as dirt and debris flew into his mouth.

The giant drill cut an enormous cavern right below the financial district. Once it stopped, a hatch opened and the Underminer emerged. He pointed a detonator at the newly carved cavern and laughed. "Consider yourselves UNDERMINED!" He pressed a button, and within seconds, there was a tremendous explosion!

Bank buildings dropped straight down to the cavern floor, sending clouds of dust into the air. The tunneler began moving again—this time drilling directly through the walls of the banks and their vaults!

BWOOP! BWOOP! BWOOP! The deafening alarms rang out from the vaults, and bright-red emergency lights flickered urgently. But none of that stopped the Underminer from his work. He pulled a long, wide tube from the tunneler and dragged it into the vaults. Planting himself in the center of the room, he turned on the powerful suction. Mountains of cash, bonds, and deeds were sucked up through the tube and into the tunneler!

Mr. Incredible appeared. With his hands on his hips, he said, "Underminer. We meet again—"

Startled, the Underminer, still holding the vacuum, turned toward him. In a flash, Mr. Incredible was sucked inside! The tube bulged and twisted as the Super's body snaked its way through.

"Oh, GREAT!" barked the Underminer, irritated. "Now *he's* on the agenda."

The pressure built as Mr. Incredible clogged the tube until the strength of it finally forced him through. He flew out the other side, tumbling into the tunneler's vault. A blizzard of coins and cash followed, falling into the piles around him.

The Underminer scowled as he heard a banging sound from deep inside the vault. A dent appeared, growing bigger and bigger with each *bang*. The

Underminer threw the controls to autopilot. Suddenly, Mr. Incredible burst through the metal wall, and the Underminer whacked him on the head! The Underminer flashed his clawlike hands and punched them up and down like jackhammers.

"INCREDIBLE!" the Underminer shouted. "Meet JACK HAMMER!"

Mr. Incredible and the Underminer fought, tumbling around the tunneler until Mr. Incredible threw the Underminer against the control panel, breaking it! The massive machine began tunneling out of control, drilling upward, toward the surface. The Underminer ducked into the vault, and it separated from the tunneler—the vault was actually an escape pod! Its miniature driller quickly burrowed into the dirt floor and vanished. Mr. Incredible was left inside the tunneler, which continued to zigzag haphazardly toward the surface.

Mr. Incredible pounded every button and flipped every switch and lever as he attempted to stop the tunneler. A screen next to the control panel blinked a message: BREACH IN THREE . . . TWO . . . ONE . . .

"No, no, no, NO NO NO NO!!!!!!" he yelled, banging his fists against the panel.

With a loud *CRASH,* the tunneler exploded through

the asphalt and burst onto the streets near the stadium parking lot!

A few blocks away, Dash was keeping the crowd back. He noticed the plume of dust in the near distance. "Stay back!" he shouted. Then, using his Super speed, he zoomed off toward the action.

Violet wanted to help, too. When she spotted Dash whipping by in a blur, she shouted, "You're not sticking me with babysitting!" She ran after Dash, pushing Jack-Jack along in his stroller. It was always a challenge to keep their baby brother *and* the city safe when a villain struck.

Elastigirl stretched, swinging across the city, making her way to the top of the tunneler. Mr. Incredible emerged from inside the machine.

"I can't steer it or stop it!" he said. "And the Underminer has escaped!"

"We'll have to stop it from—" Elastigirl's eyes widened as she noticed the monorail approaching. It was too late. The tunneler slammed into a column holding up the tracks! The tracks crumbled apart and the train began to dive toward the ground. Just then, an icy breeze swept in. It was Frozone! The newly arrived Super used his ice powers to create a track that guided the monorail smoothly out of harm's way.

But the tunneler continued its destruction through the city.

"We have to stop this thing before it gets to the overpass!" shouted Elastigirl.

"I'll try and keep it away from the buildings!" Mr. Incredible yelled back as he jammed a lamppost into the treads of the tunneler. But the enormous machine kept going, scraping against the sides of buildings and crushing anything in its path.

As Dash raced through the scattered debris, the tunneler flung a car into the air. He swiftly swept an older woman out of the way.

"Thank you so much, young man—" she said.

Dash saw Jack-Jack rolling toward him in his stroller, giggling and babbling. Dash grunted, realizing the responsibility of babysitting was back on him. Now he was responsible for keeping Jack-Jack safe while also fighting the forces of evil!

"Violet!" he shouted, knowing his sister was hiding somewhere nearby with her power of invisibility. But he stayed focused, always up for a challenge.

Violet reappeared and shielded herself with force fields as she chased after the tunneler. Mr. Incredible continued to struggle, using all his strength to try to stop the machine.

Elastigirl swung her way up to the overpass and stretched her arms in both directions, stopping cars from entering the bridge as the tunneler took down its supports. The bridge collapsed, and Elastigirl stretched to grab a streetlight, pulling herself to safety.

Mr. Incredible jammed a fallen pole into the tunneler's treads, stopping the machine only for a moment before it snapped the pole in half. Dash blurred past him.

"Heads up, Dad!" he yelled. Suddenly, Mr. Incredible found himself holding Jack-Jack!

Violet threw force fields on the other side of the tunneler to protect bystanders.

Elastigirl saw her. "VIOLET? WHO'S WATCHING JACK-JACK?"

"Dash is watching him!" answered Violet.

Mr. Incredible sprinted past Violet and handed her Jack-Jack. "Violet, here! You take him!"

Elastigirl leaped down from a streetlight and flipped into the open hatch of the tunneler.

As Mr. Incredible and the kids chased after the tunneler, they noticed what was sitting directly in its path: city hall. They climbed up to the hatch and hurried inside.

Elastigirl snaked her body through the tunneler's

machinery, stretching to her limits, trying to spill the engine's coolant to force it to overheat. Mr. Incredible appeared.

"Help me with the boiler!" Elastigirl urged. He rushed in to help her pry it loose, toppling it over. "That should do it!" She turned to go—and saw her children standing there. Panicking, she screamed, "What are you kids doing? GET OUTTA HERE! This thing's gonna blow!"

"THERE'S NO TIME!" shouted Violet. She handed Jack-Jack to her mom and created a force field around the family just as a massive boom rippled throughout the tunneler. The giant machine stalled—right in front of city hall! The Incredibles huddled together on the floor of the tunneler, laughing with relief.

"We did it!" cheered Dash.

"Freeze, Supers!" The family looked up through the open hatch to see a team of cops with their weapons drawn and aimed at them.

"Ahh, what did we do?" said Mr. Incredible.

2

Agent Rick Dicker from the National Supers Agency drove the Incredibles home. The family, now back in their regular clothes, sat silently listening to the hum of the armored police van's motor.

"Well, that went poorly," said Mr. Incredible, finally breaking the silence.

"Dad—" Violet said softly. "This is probably not the best time to tell you, but something else happened today . . . with a kid . . . and my mask. . . ." She told Bob that Tony had seen her.

They soon pulled into the parking lot of their current home: the Safari Court Motel. The small brown-and-orange motel had a sign above it with lights that flickered weakly. When the rear doors of the van opened, the Parr family poured out. Helen and the kids slowly walked toward their room as Bob lingered behind to tell Dicker about Violet's incident with Tony.

"Talkative type?" asked Dicker through the van window.

"Don't know. Last name is Rydinger," answered Bob.

Dicker whipped out a pad and scribbled down the name. Then he told Bob he would check it out.

Bob moved off to join Helen and the kids, but Dicker called him back. "Bob, Helen . . . ? A word, if you don't mind?" Dicker's face fell as they approached the van. "The program's been shut down," he said with a sigh. He knew how important the Super Relocation Program was to the Parr family. Ever since Supers were forced underground, it had helped them many times. "Politicians don't understand people who do good simply because it's right. Makes 'em nervous. They've been gunnin' for Supers for years. Today was all they needed. . . ." His voice trailed off. His sad eyes said it all: he genuinely felt bad about the whole situation. "Anyway . . . I'm done. I'm afraid two more weeks in the motel is the best I can do for ya. It ain't much."

"You've done plenty, Rick," said Helen, grateful. She leaned in and gave him a hug through the window.

"We won't forget," said Bob.

"Well, it has been a great honor workin' with you good people," said Dicker.

Bob and Helen thanked him for all he had done and wished him luck. Then they waved and watched the van go.

Later that night, the Parr family sat down to dinner around a small, round table. It had been months since they'd moved in, and the motel room felt cluttered and crowded. It wasn't nearly big enough for a family of five.

Several cartons of Chinese takeout sat in the center of the table as they prepared to eat. Helen placed Jack-Jack in his high chair and clicked the buckle around his waist. Dash reached for the egg rolls, but Violet created a force field around the food and quickly asked, "Did you wash your hands?"

He scowled and raced from the table in a blur. In a flash he was back, reaching for the egg rolls again.

Violet protected the egg rolls with another force field and asked, "With soap?"

Dash zipped off again, returning within seconds.

"Did you dry them?" she asked, grinning.

Dash narrowed his eyes and speed-shook his hands. Then, with a triumphant grunt, he finally grabbed an egg roll. He looked in the rest of the cartons and frowned. "Is this all vegetables?" he asked. "Who ordered all vegetables?"

"I did," said Helen. Her strict tone said she wasn't up for hearing complaints. "They're good, and you're going to have some," she added, serving him a heaping portion.

"Are we going to talk about the elephant in the room?" asked Violet.

Bob looked up at Violet with his mouth full of stir-fried beans. "What?" he asked.

"The elephant in the room," repeated Violet.

"What elephant?" asked Bob, clueless.

"I guess not, then," said Violet.

"You're referring to today," said Helen.

"Yeah, what's the deal with today?" asked Dash.

"We all made mistakes," said Helen calmly. "For example, you kids were supposed to watch Jack-Jack."

"Babysitting," said Violet, annoyed. "While you guys did the important stuff."

"We talked about this," said Helen. "You're not old enough to decide about these things—"

"We are old enough to help out," Violet interrupted. Dash agreed as Violet turned to her father. "Isn't that what you tell us, Dad?"

Bob looked down at his food. "Yeah, well, 'help out' can mean many different things. . . ."

"But we're supposed to help if there's trouble . . . ," said Violet.

"Well . . . yeah, but—" Bob stammered.

"Aren't you glad we helped today?" asked Violet.

"Well, yeah. I was—AM—" said Bob, stumbling as he tried to find the right words.

"We wanna fight bad guys!" exclaimed Dash.

Jack-Jack babbled in approval and raised his fists, then slammed them down on the tray of his high chair.

"No—you don't!" said Helen, finally weighing in.

Violet turned to Helen. "You said things were different now."

Helen explained that they *were* different when they were on the island with Syndrome. The rules weren't the same because they were all in danger, but since they were now back at home, everything was supposed to be normal again.

"So now we've gotta go back to never using our powers?" said Violet angrily.

"It defines who I am," said Dash.

"We're not saying you have—" Bob looked at Dash as his son's words registered. "What?"

"Someone on TV said it," replied Dash, shrugging it off.

"Can—can we just eat? The dinner? While it's—hot?" asked Helen, wishing the conversation would just stop.

"Did we do something wrong?" asked Dash.

"Yes," said Helen.

"No," said Bob. Helen gave Bob a sharp look, but Bob refused to agree with her. *"We didn't do anything wrong,"* he insisted.

"Superheroes ARE illegal," said Helen. "Whether it's fair or not, that's the law."

"The law should be fair," said Bob. "What are we teaching our kids?"

"To respect the law!" replied Helen, getting heated.

"Even when the law is disrespectful?"

"If laws are unjust, there are laws to change them—otherwise it's chaos!"

"Which is exactly what we have!" boomed Bob.

Frustrated, Helen slammed her hand on the table, causing the plates to bounce and rattle. Everyone froze, stunned by her outburst. The awkward moment of silence seemed to linger before everyone slowly resumed eating.

Then Violet said softly, "I just thought it was kind of cool."

"What was?" asked Helen calmly.

"Fighting crime. As a family," she answered.

Everyone exchanged glances, and without a word they knew: they all agreed.

"It was cool," said Helen. "But it's over. The world is what it is. We have to . . . adapt."

"Are things . . . bad?" asked Dash, concerned.

"Things are fine," answered Helen.

Happy to hear those words, Dash cleared his mind of the whole conversation and asked to be excused. In a matter of seconds he cleared his plate, turned on the television, and settled onto the couch to watch a giant Japanese monster attack a city.

Violet got up and turned to Bob. "How much longer in the motel?" she asked.

Bob stammered, unsure of how to answer. He looked over at Helen.

"Not much longer, honey," said Helen. She forced a smile, trying to hide the weight of the big question that hung in her mind: Where would they go next?

After the kids were asleep, Helen and Bob sat outside by the small motel pool, staring at the rippling reflection of the moonlight on the water, deep in thought.

"What are we gonna do?" asked Helen.

"I don't know," said Bob with a shrug. "Maybe Dicker'll find something—"

"Dicker is done, Bob," Helen said. "Any thought we had about being Supers again is fantasy. One of us has gotta get a job."

Helen said she knew that Bob's job at the insurance company had been hard on him. She suggested that maybe it was her turn to get a job and he could stay home and take care of the kids.

"NO," said Bob. "I'm the breadwinner. I'll start . . .

winning some bread tomorrow." He sighed. "You know where my suit and ties are?"

"Burned up when—" Helen started.

"—the jet destroyed our house," Bob said along with her as he recalled the obvious truth. The two smiled at each other, trying to remember to appreciate the fact that they had all made it through that awful day.

Helen gently rested her hand on top of his as she reminded him that they couldn't count on anyone but themselves. Just then, they heard a noise as a shadowy silhouette approached, watching them from the other side of the pool. Helen and Bob stood up defensively. The figure stepped into the light—it was their good friend Lucius.

After breathing a sigh of relief, Bob frowned at him. "Well, where'd YOU go today?" he said. "I noticed you missed all the fun," he added sarcastically.

"Don't be mad because I know when to leave a party," said Lucius. "I'm just as illegal as you guys. Besides, I knew the cops would let you go."

Helen smiled. "Yeah, in spite of Bob's best efforts."

Bob rolled his eyes and smirked at her comment.

"I heard the program shut down," said Lucius. "How much longer you in this motel?"

"Two weeks," said Bob.

"Now, you know the offer still stands," said Lucius.

"You're very generous, but there are five of us," said Helen. "We wouldn't do that to you and Honey," said Helen.

"Door's always open," said Lucius. Then he told them about a man he had met on his way home from the Underminer attack. He pulled out a business card and handed it to Helen. He explained that the man represented a business tycoon named Winston Deavor, who wanted to meet the three of them to talk about "hero stuff." Lucius opened his coat, revealing that he was wearing his Frozone Supersuit.

"Aw, geez," groaned Helen. "More Superhero trouble? We just came from the police station, Lucius."

Bob looked up at his friend and grinned. "When?" he asked.

"Tonight. I'm going there now."

"You enjoy," said Helen. "I'm sittin' this one out."

Lucius explained that Deavor wanted to see all three of them.

Bob turned to Helen. "Let's just at least hear what he has to say."

Helen sighed. Then she nodded, slowly surrendering

to the pressure. Bob beamed, thoroughly excited at the prospect of discussing hero stuff.

"Go . . . in our Supersuits?" asked Helen.

"Yeah, might want to wear the old Supersuits," said Lucius. "Got a feeling he's nostalgic."

4

Mr. Incredible, Elastigirl, and Frozone soon arrived in a town car in front of DevTech headquarters. The modern skyscraper seemed to stretch up into the clouds. As they stepped out of the car, the driver handed each of them a security badge. Then he ushered them through the revolving door and into the building.

The sleek glass elevator rose to the top floor, offering an incredible view of the city below. When the doors opened, a man took their coats and led them into the enormous penthouse.

"I LOVE SUPERHEROES!" said a lively voice behind them. They turned to see Winston Deavor, beaming as he trotted down a curved staircase. "The powers, the costumes, the mythic struggles . . . ," he said as he crossed over to them. He introduced himself and shook their hands, enthusiastically singing each of their theme songs.

"I can't tell you what a thrill this is," said Winston as a woman entered the room. He gestured toward her. "And this is my tardy sister, Evelyn."

"Hello there, Superheroes," she said. "I'm late." She turned to Winston and added, "I'm scolding myself so you don't have to."

Winston shot her a disapproving look and then turned back to the Supers, admiring their suits. "Spectacular," he said. "Sporting the old suits from yesteryear, not the ones you wore earlier today with your kids."

Mr. Incredible and Elastigirl swapped a look, visibly shaken by the fact that Winston Deavor knew their children.

He quickly responded. "You're uncomfortable that I know your alter egos—that you two are married and have kids." He told them they had nothing to worry about. "You probably don't remember me," he added, "but I worked for Rick Dicker for a short period, right before you all went underground."

Frozone studied his face, and something suddenly

clicked. "Yeah!" he said, recapturing the image in his mind. "Long hair?"

Winston nodded. "Dicker made me cut it. My father was SO proud that I was even remotely connected to you guys." Looking over at a portrait of his father hanging on the wall, Winston explained that he had adored Supers. "He donated to Superhero causes, he raised money for the Dynaguy statue in Avery Park. . . ." Winston's thoughts drifted to his parent's admiration. "He got to know Supers personally, even installed a phone with direct lines to Gazerbeam and Fironic in case of emergencies. He loved that, showed it off to everyone. . . ." Winston's voice trailed off as he paused for a moment, enjoying the fond memory. Then he snapped back to the conversation and fixed his gaze on the Supers. "He was heartbroken when you were all forced to go underground," he said.

"Father believed the world would become more dangerous without you," added Evelyn.

"He didn't know how right he was," said Winston. Then he shared a painful event from their childhood. One night, someone had broken into their family's home. "My mother wanted to hide, but my father insisted they call Gazerbeam—on the direct line. No answer. He called Fironic; no answer. Superheroes had just been made illegal, but somehow he was sure they'd answer his call. The robbers discovered him on the phone . . . and shot him."

"Must have been hard," said Elastigirl.

"Especially for Mother," said Evelyn. "She died a few months later. Heartbreak."

"If Superheroes had not been forced underground, it never would have happened. I'm sure of it," said Winston.

"Or . . . Dad could've taken Mom to the safe room as soon as he knew—" added Evelyn, a tinge of irritation to her voice.

"I disagree *strongly,*" Winston interrupted. "But we're not going into it right now," he added, his tone becoming light again. He turned to the Supers. "We've had this argument forever. Pay no attention. The point is—we picked ourselves up and put our energy into building DevTech."

"A world-class telecommunications company," said Frozone.

"Perfectly positioned to make some wrong things right. Hence this meeting!" said Winston.

Moments later, Mr. Incredible, Elastigirl, and Frozone were seated on a couch inside a screening room. Winston stood before them as Evelyn shut the blinds. "Let me ask you something. What is the main reason you were all forced underground?"

"Ignorance," Mr. Incredible answered quickly.

"Perception," said Winston.

Evelyn clicked a button on a remote, and footage from the Underminer attack appeared on a wall-sized screen. "Take today, for example, with the Underminer. Difficult situation. You were faced with a lot of hard decisions."

"Ah, tell me about it," said Mr. Incredible.

"I can't," said Winston. He leaned in dramatically. "Because I didn't see it." The Supers exchanged glances. "Neither did anyone else. So when you fight bad guys—like today—people don't see the fight or what led up to it. They see what politicians tell them to see: they see destruction, and they see you." Winston paused before continuing. "You know what they don't see? This—"

Footage of a woman speaking to a camera appeared. "My car was headed over the edge, and suddenly, I felt this arm wrapping around me and pulling me out of my window to safety," the woman said. "Elastigirl saved my life," she added gratefully.

"Yeah, you're darn straight, she did!" said Mr. Incredible.

The footage paused, freezing on the image, and Winston turned to the Supers. "If we want to change people's perceptions about Superheroes, we need *you* to share *your* perceptions with the world."

"How do we do that?" asked Elastigirl.

Evelyn put three separate images on the screen. Two of them showed different angles of Elastigirl's face, and one showed Winston. It was footage from just minutes before. On the screen, Winston said, "We need *you* to share *your* perceptions with the world."

Then Elastigirl asked her question. "How do we do that?"

Evelyn clicked the remote again, and a live feed appeared on the screen, showing the three Supers' faces. Simultaneously, they looked down at the security badges clipped to their suits. "With cameras," said Evelyn. She explained that they would sew tiny cameras into the fabric of their Supersuits.

Elastigirl was impressed. "That is so cool," she said, inspecting the badge. She looked up at the screen, admiring the crystal clear images. "So small, and the picture is outstanding."

Evelyn thanked her for the compliment. "Designed 'em myself."

"Well, that's fantastic," said Mr. Incredible, getting

more and more excited. "The public needs to be in our shoes."

"All we need now are the Superest Superheroes. We need you three!" said Winston enthusiastically.

"But our family just had a run-in with the law," said Elastigirl, bringing them all back to reality. "I can't risk that happening again."

"Understood—but do you change your kids to fit into a smaller world, or do you make the world larger *for* your kids?" asked Winston. "We've got resources, lobbyists, worldwide connections, and, most important, insurance."

"Insurance is key," said Mr. Incredible.

Winston explained that it would be their top priority. "You just be Super, and we'll get the public on your side. We won't stop until you're all legal again," he said.

"This sounds GREAT!" said Mr. Incredible. He slapped his hands together. "Let's say we're all in— what's my first assignment?"

"That enthusiasm is golden," Winston replied. "Hold on to it. But for our first move, Elastigirl is our best play."

As Winston extended a hand to Elastigirl, Mr. Incredible stood, completely stunned, as if he had just been punched in the gut. "Better than . . . me?" he asked, finally getting out a few words. Elastigirl cleared her throat and glared at her husband, and he stammered, "I mean, she's good. She's—uh—really a credit to her—uh, but . . . I mean, you know?"

Winston smiled at Mr. Incredible. "With great respect, let's not test the whole 'insurance will pay for everything' idea on the first go-round, okay?" he said gently, trying not to offend him.

Frozone clenched his lips together, trying to hold back the laughter that wanted to blast out of his mouth.

"Wait a minute—you're saying, what, I'm . . . messy?" said Mr. Incredible, still trying to process what was happening.

Winston handed Mr. Incredible a folder. He looked at it, bewildered, as Winston explained that Evelyn had compared the costs and benefits of their last five years of crime fighting. "Elastigirl's numbers are self-explanatory," he said.

Mr. Incredible shifted his weight uncomfortably. "Well, it's not a fair comparison . . . ," he said, feeling the need to defend himself. "Heavyweight problems need heavyweight solutions."

Winston smiled. "Of course, we'll solve all kinds

of problems together, after the perfect launch with Elastigirl," he said brightly, wrapping up the meeting.

Evelyn turned to Elastigirl. "So, whaddya say?" she asked.

All eyes turned to Elastigirl, waiting for her response. "What do I say?" she said, stalling and looking over at Mr. Incredible. She chuckled. "I don't know."

5

Bob sat up in bed later that night, frowning as Helen brushed her teeth in the bathroom. He cringed with every *swoosh* of her toothbrush and finally called out the question he had been stewing about since they'd left the Deavors. "Whaddya mean you *don't know?* A few hours before, you were saying it was over and being a Superhero was a fantasy! Now you get the offer of a lifetime and you *don't know!*"

"It's not that simple, Bob," Helen said. "I want to protect the kids—"

"So do I!" he blurted.

"—from jail, Bob!" Helen said, spitting a mouthful of toothpaste into the sink.

"And how do you do that?" he asked. "By turning

down a chance to change the law that forces them to hide what they are?"

Helen put down her toothbrush and walked into the bedroom, irritated by Bob's refusal to understand where she was coming from. "They haven't decided what they are!" she yelled. "They're still kids—"

"Kids with powers, which makes them Supers—whether they decide to use those powers or not!" said Bob, firmly planted in his opinion. "This will benefit them!"

"Maybe. In twenty years," Helen said, climbing into bed. "It's not a good time to be away," she said. "Dash is having trouble with homework. Vi is worried about her first date with that boy she likes—Tony. And Jack-Jack . . ." Her voice trailed off.

Bob looked at her, waiting for her to finish the sentence. "Jack-Jack?" he said, prompting her to continue. "What's wrong with him?"

"Okay, nothing is wrong with Jack-Jack," she said. "But even a normal baby needs a lot of attention. I'm just not sure I can leave."

"Of course you can leave!" said Bob, exasperated. "You've got to! So that I—we—can be Supers again! So our kids can have that choice!"

"So YOU can have that choice," Helen said with a chuckle.

"All right—yes," said Bob, admitting the truth. "So I can have that choice. And I would do a GREAT job, regardless of what Winston's pie charts say." He paused. "But they want you." He took a deep breath as his face twisted up, trying to spit out his words. "And you'll . . . do a great—job. Too."

Helen stared at him, taking note of his miserable expression and tone. "Well, that was excruciating to watch," she said with a smile.

Bob laughed.

"I can't lie to you—it's nice to be wanted," she confessed. "To be taken seriously again after all this time. Flattering, you know? But . . ." She sighed as she tossed the idea over in her mind.

"What's the choice?" said Bob, feeling like he was pointing out the obvious. "One: Do this right, get paid well, we're out of the motel, and things get better for all Supers—including our kids. Or two: I find a job in two weeks or we're homeless."

Helen knew what he was saying made sense, but she was still uncertain about whether it was the right thing to do. "You know it's crazy, right?" she said. "To help my family, I gotta leave it; to fix the law, I gotta break it."

"You'll be great," said Bob.

"I know I will," said Helen. "But what about you? We have kids."

"I'll watch the kids, no problem. Easy," said Bob.

Helen grinned. "Easy, huh?" she said, taking his hand. "You're adorable. Well, if there IS a problem, I'll drop this thing and come right back—"

"You won't need to," said Bob. "I got it. You go, do this thing." He rolled over, ready to get to sleep. "Do it so"—he paused and grinned—"I can do it better."

Helen playfully hit him with her pillow. They said good night, knowing that in the morning she would call Winston to give him the news: Elastigirl was in.

6

A couple days later, the Parr family sat inside a limousine as it drove them over lush rolling hills and toward their new home. Helen spoke with Winston on the phone.

"We're partners now," he said. "Can't have my partners livin' in a motel."

"But who—whose house—is it a house?" Helen asked. Just then, up on a hill, an enormous modern mansion came into view. Dash's jaw dropped as he took in the sight of it. It was a far cry from the Safari Court Motel.

"It's my house," said Winston. "I have several; I'm not using that one. Stay as long as you need."

"I don't know what to say," said Helen, shocked.

"How about thanks!" said Bob.

They hopped out of the limo and rushed to the front door. As it swung open, the family stood for a moment, staring. With its high ceilings, massive boulders, indoor fountains, and waterfalls, it looked like the luxurious lair of a high-profile spy.

"THIS . . . is our new house?" said Dash, beyond thrilled.

"Okay, easy, tiger—it's being loaned to us," said Helen as they slowly made their way through, looking around.

"Ehhh, this is . . . homey," said Violet sarcastically, not nearly as taken as Dash.

"I mean, look at this place," said Bob. "Winston bought it from an eccentric billionaire who liked to come and go without being seen, so the house has multiple hidden exits."

Eager to explore, Dash zoomed away.

"Good thing we won't stand out," said Violet, her voice still dripping with sarcasm. "Wouldn't want to attract any unnecessary attention."

"IT'S GOT A BIG YARD!" screamed Dash from outside.

Helen turned to Bob, a little uncertain. "This is . . . Isn't this a bit much?"

"NEAR A FOREST!" added Dash.

"Would you rather be at the motel?" Bob asked, knowing the answer.

"AND A POOL!" shouted Dash. They heard a loud SPLASH as Dash did a cannonball into the pool.

"What exactly IS Mom's new job?" asked Violet.

Instead of answering the question, Bob reminded her that they were out of the motel.

Dash zipped back in, soaking wet, with a huge smile on his face. He shook himself dry, like a dog. Then he noticed a remote control hanging on the wall. He grabbed it and started pressing random buttons. Suddenly, a deep humming came from beneath the house as sections of the floor began to separate! The sections pulled apart like pieces of a puzzle, revealing more fountains and hidden streams. Dash pressed another button and more secret panels parted, unveiling a secret waterfall! The water spilled from the ceiling and dropped in rolling patterns, falling into hidden pools beneath the floor.

"WICKED COOL!" he exclaimed.

Just then, a large couch began to tumble into one of the streams in the floor. Dash panicked and poked at the button again—and the floor started closing on the couch, crushing it! Bob and Helen shouted at him and he nervously pressed more buttons, but the floors continued to open and close, bashing the couch. Finally, Dash gave up, chucking the remote and running off.

Later that day, Bob held Jack-Jack as Elastigirl emerged from the bathroom wearing the new Supersuit the Deavors had sent. It was a shiny gray, and patterned with light black scales.

"This isn't me . . . ," she said, looking at herself in a full-length mirror. She turned, assessing the suit from different angles. "I'm not all dark and angsty. I'm Elastigirl! I'm, ya know, flexible!"

"E designed this?" asked Bob.

"No, some guy named Alexander Galbaki," she answered.

Bob burst out laughing at the thought of Edna seeing Elastigirl wearing another designer's suit. He knew she'd be furious. "Glad it's you and not me. 'Cause you're gonna hear from her." Then he handed her a card that had come with the Supersuit.

In neat handwriting, it read *Elastigirl, there's an accessory in the garage. —Evelyn*

Minutes later, Elastigirl and Bob entered the garage and saw a gleaming, high-tech red motorcycle. Clearly designed specifically for her, it was made of two separate unicycles, powered by a small rocket.

Elastigirl's eyes lit up. "A new Elasticycle . . . ," she said.

"I didn't know you had a bike," said Bob, surprised.

"Hey, I had a Mohawk," she said. "There's a lot about me you don't know." Elastigirl sat on the bike and felt a rush of excitement. She activated the handles and it sparked to life, humming with power. A message appeared on the dashboard: HOPE YOU LIKE IT! —E.D.

She gave it a little gas and it roared, spinning around in a tight circle. She hopped on one leg as it swerved into a wall. "WHOA, WHOA—WHOA! OHHH!" she shrieked. She stopped the bike. "Eh, I'll get the hang of it."

"You will be great," said Bob.

"I will be great," she said. "And you will, too."

"We will both be great," said Bob, smiling confidently.

They said goodbye and Bob pressed a button on the wall. The garage door slid open and a thin waterfall rushed down, dividing the garage and the beautiful landscape outside. Elastigirl hit the accelerator and the waterfall created a hole that she zoomed through. Feeling a mixture of pride and envy, Bob stood holding

Jack-Jack as he watched her race out onto the open road.

The next morning, he prepared breakfast for the kids. Jack-Jack sat in his high chair, shoving cereal into his mouth and dropping a lot on the floor. Dash started to fill a bowl with a sugary cereal called Sugar Bombs, but Bob grabbed the box out of his hands. "No Sugar Bombs on my watch." Dash grumbled as Bob replaced the sugary cereal with a more reasonable box of Fiber O's.

Dash shrugged and asked where his mother was as he held up a spoonful of the bland cereal.

"She's up and out," answered Bob. "She's at her new job doing hero work."

"But I thought Superheroes were still illegal," said Violet.

"They are," said Bob. "For now," he added.

"So Mom is getting paid to break the law," Violet said, amazed that neither of her parents saw anything wrong with this idea.

"She's an advocate for Superheroes," said Bob, trying to make it sound good. "It's a new job."

"So Mom is going out, illegally, to explain why she shouldn't be illegal," said Violet.

Bob squirmed and looked out the window as he

tried to think of how to get Violet to see it his way. He brightened when he saw the school bus arrive. "The bus is here!" he cheered.

With Super speed, Dash finished his cereal, refilled a second bowl with Sugar Bombs, wolfed it down, and grabbed his backpack. Violet headed for the door. Bob stuffed a textbook into Dash's backpack before he raced out.

Relieved, Bob lifted Jack-Jack out of his high chair and cooed, "Oh, we're gonna get along just fine, 'cause you don't ask any hard questions."

Jack-Jack giggled and babbled happily.

7

Violet got ready that night for her date with Tony as Bob tried to put Jack-Jack to bed. He sat in an easy chair with Jack-Jack resting on his chest, sleepily sucking on a bottle. Bob read him a bedtime story, and once Jack-Jack's head started to droop, Bob carefully closed the book, rose, and put him in his crib. Then he tiptoed out of the room and downstairs.

Bob collapsed onto the couch and got ready to watch some television. As he settled comfortably and clicked on the remote, Dash appeared, holding up his math textbook. Bob sighed and clicked off the television. He got off the couch and dragged himself over to sit with Dash at the kitchen table.

Bob squinted as he read through the problems in

the textbook and then reached for a pencil. He sat sweating. He scrawled some math equations across a piece of scrap paper.

"That's not the way you're supposed to do it, Dad," said Dash, pointing to the solved problem in the book.

"I don't know that way," snapped Bob. "Why would they change math? Math is math! MATH IS MATH!"

"Ehh—it's okay, Dad," said Dash, letting his father off the hook. "I'll just wait for Mom to get back."

"What?" asked Bob, offended. "Well, she won't understand it any better than I do—" The television suddenly blared from the other room. He went into the family room, startled to find Jack-Jack sitting on the couch, using the remote to flip through the channels!

Bob took Jack-Jack back upstairs. He sat in the recliner and read the bedtime story to the baby again. Bob sank lower and lower into the comfortable recliner until his head drooped to the side and he fell asleep. Jack-Jack slapped him in the face a couple times to wake him up and start the story again.

Elastigirl sat on her cycle in New Urbem. She watched as a crowd gathered in the center of the city, waiting to see the unveiling of a new hovertrain. The mayor appeared at a podium and proudly gave a speech as he prepared to cut the ribbon and declare the train open to the public.

The Deavors sat nearby in a remote editing suite. They watched the live footage from Elastigirl's suitcam on monitors and communicated with her through a headset.

In an effort to find crimes to stop, the Deavors had suggested she listen to the police scanner that was connected to her cycle. Even though she wasn't crazy about the idea, she turned up the volume on the scanner.

"Are you sure the police are gonna be okay with this?" Elastigirl whispered into her headset.

"Sure, you're making life easy for them," replied Evelyn.

"They still haven't forgiven us for the last time we made life easy for them," said Elastigirl.

"With all due respect," said Evelyn, "if YOU had handled the Underminer, things would have been different."

Elastigirl chuckled.

"I'm just saying," Evelyn added.

The mayor continued his speech. "But I am happy

to report that we are here today ahead of schedule, to launch our magnificent new hovertrain. It can get you where you need to go at ridiculous speeds. The future is open for business!"

The mayor cut the ribbon with a giant pair of scissors, and the crowd cheered. While a live band played boisterous music and a storm of flashbulbs went off, the doors to the hovertrain slid open. Passengers poured inside and the train rose up, hovering over the track. It began to pull out of the station, but then suddenly, it stopped, dropping back onto the track with a loud thud.

The crowd murmured, confused, as the train slowly rose above the track again. Uncertain applause filled the station, and the train began to move . . . but it was going backward! As the train accelerated, the crowd's excitement turned to terror.

"It's going in the wrong direction!" Elastigirl shouted. She took off on her Elasticycle, and it moved with her every stretch, separating and coming together as she tried to catch up to the high-speed train. "This thing's really movin'!" she said. "Two hundred and climbing! How much track has been built?"

"About twenty-five miles," answered Evelyn.

"No one can shut this thing down?" asked Elastigirl.

"They've tried! No go!" urged Evelyn.

"Overrides?" asked Elastigirl.

"They're locked out of the system!" said Evelyn.

Elastigirl's mind raced as she tried to think of a way to stop the train. She knew the chances of her catching up to it were slim at best. "What about a fail-safe?"

"Not enough time!"

"Someone's calling!" said Elastigirl. "Switching over!" Elastigirl picked up her phone—it was Dash asking if she knew where his favorite sneakers were. In the background, she could hear Bob yelling, "DO NOT CALL YOUR MOTHER!"

"Dash, honey?" said Elastigirl. "Now's not a good time to talk!" She told him she would call him back, then switched back to Evelyn. "How much time?"

"Less than two minutes," Evelyn answered.

Elastigirl rode through tunnels and onto rooftops, trying to catch up to the train, until she finally managed to land directly on top of it. But before she could figure out her next move, she saw a tunnel approaching! She hopped off her cycle, sending it crashing into the side of the mountain as she flattened herself on top of the train. Elastigirl clung to it as it made its way through the tunnel. She crawled to the back of the train and and saw the engineer staring straight ahead. He didn't blink or move a muscle when she banged on the windshield, trying to get his attention.

Just as the train was about to race off the track, Elastigirl stretched herself into a parachute to slow it down. The train busted through a construction barricade and finally came to a stop as it dangled over the end of the tracks!

Elastigirl ran through the cabin, checking on the passengers. "Is everybody all right? Is anybody injured?" she asked as she hurried through. Her eyes moved to the opposite end of the train, where she noticed an odd pulsing light coming from the engineer's cabin. She headed toward it.

Kicking down the door, she burst in and found the engineer blinking his eyes, as if coming back to consciousness. "Your story better be good!" she said, helping him to his feet. Then she slapped him in the face to wake him up.

"Uh, where am I?" asked the engineer, dazed.

A message flashed on the large monitor in the train's control panel: WELCOME BACK, ELASTIGIRL. —THE SCREENSLAVER

Then the screen went black.

8

For what felt like the hundredth time, Bob lowered Jack-Jack into his crib and turned off the reading lamp. The soft glow of the nightlight made the baby look peaceful and sweet. Bob lingered, staring for a moment, then flipped a table upside down and placed it over the crib. Determined to keep Jack-Jack from climbing out, he put a stack of books on top of the table before heading downstairs.

On his way to the couch, Bob noticed Violet sitting with her head down. She had never left for her date.

"Honey, why are you—" he started.

"DON'T say anything," said Violet, cutting him off.

Bob watched in silence as Violet trudged off to her bedroom.

A moment later, he knocked on her door. "Are you okay?" he asked.

"I'm fine," said Violet, her voice sounding flat and irritated. "I don't want to talk about it."

"Tony didn't even call?" Bob asked gently.

"I DON'T wanna talk about it," repeated Violet. Bob tried to say something else, but Violet interrupted again. "Dad! If you want me to feel better, then leave me alone. Please?" Her voice cracked.

Bob tried to think of something comforting to say but unable to, he stood silently. Finally, he headed back down to the family room. Before he reached the bottom of the stairs, he heard the television. His face dropped as he entered to find Jack-Jack, once again, sitting on the couch, holding the remote, flicking through channels!

Finally surrendering, Bob sat beside Jack-Jack and soon fell asleep. Jack-Jack sucked on his bottle and watched an old crime movie. Bob snored away as Jack-Jack took in every detail. A masked robber held a shop owner at gunpoint and cleaned out his cash register. Fully enthralled by the drama, Jack-Jack climbed down from the couch and crawled closer to the television, sitting right in front of it.

He turned to look at the sliding-glass door and saw

a raccoon rummaging through the garbage can in the backyard. He looked at the masked robber digging through the cash register on television and then back at the raccoon. He frowned. The raccoon noticed Jack-Jack staring and let out a fierce hiss, showing off its sharp teeth. Jack-Jack babbled at it angrily.

The raccoon turned its attention back to the half-eaten chicken leg it had taken from the garbage can. Jack-Jack toddled to the door and pressed his hands against the glass . . . then passed right through it! Standing on his little feet, he grabbed the chicken leg from the raccoon and tossed it back into the garbage can. *CLANG!* He used his mind to make the lid float into the air and back onto the can.

Jack-Jack unleashed multiple Super powers as he took on the raccoon, wrestling, punching, and kicking it. He giggled as laser beams suddenly came out of his eyes and shot at the raccoon. Trying to escape the lasers, the raccoon jumped onto the patio umbrella and clung to it. The umbrella snapped closed, trapping the raccoon inside. Jack-Jack pointed his lasers at the umbrella's pole, slicing it in half! The raccoon tumbled into Jack-Jack just as the baby Superhero turned goopy and sticky. The raccoon was stuck to him, unable to move!

CRASH! Bob was awakened by the loud noises on the patio. He saw Jack-Jack and the raccoon brawling in the backyard and rushed outside to stop the fight. When he reached for Jack-Jack, the baby displayed another Super power—he multiplied! Suddenly, there were a half-dozen Jack-Jacks all over the yard!

"No, no, no! NO! NO! NO! NO!" Bob screamed as he tried to scoop up all the babies. Then each one vibrated and merged back into a single Jack-Jack. The raccoon paused before taking off. It fixed its gaze on Jack-Jack and let out a long hiss, crinkling its nose and baring its teeth. Jack-Jack giggled at it, waving his fist in the air.

"You . . . have . . . POWERS! Yeah, BABY!" Bob cheered. He inspected Jack-Jack. "And there's not a scratch on you!" He looked at the sliding-glass door and remembered he had unlocked it to get outside. "Did you go through the locked door?" he asked, laughing loudly. "Who can multiply like rabbits and go right through any . . . solid . . . Oh . . . my God." The consequences of Jack-Jack's powers finally settled in, and Bob realized how disastrous it could be. Before he spiraled into full panic mode, the phone rang.

He picked it up. "Hello?" he said.

It was Helen calling from her hotel room. Bob tried

to hide his shock and confusion over what he had just witnessed. Jack-Jack babbled in the background and Bob set him on the floor.

"Sounds like I just woke you up," said Helen.

"No, no, it's just—Jack-Jack—"

"He had an accident!" said Helen, cutting him off. "I knew it! I'm coming home right now. I never should've—"

"No, no! No accident. Stay there and finish your mission," said Bob. "And you 'never should've' what? You don't think I can do this?" He was suddenly defensive.

"Sorry," said Helen. "I misspoke." She took a breath. "Do you need me to come back?" she asked.

"No, no, no," said Bob. "I've got this. Everything's GREAT."

"What happened with Jack-Jack?" Helen asked.

"Nothing. He's in excellent health," answered Bob.

Violet marched into the room, sobbing quietly.

Helen asked Bob about Violet's date. "Uh . . ." He stalled as he watched Violet head straight for the fridge with her head down. She methodically removed a tub of ice cream from the freezer, grabbed a big spoon from the silverware drawer, and trudged back upstairs, still weeping. "Good. All fine and . . . good," he said quickly.

"And Jack-Jack went down with no trouble?" Helen asked.

Bob turned to see Jack-Jack pressed against the sliding-glass door, glaring at the raccoon. It had returned and was hissing at Jack-Jack. "Fine. Yes. No trouble," he said, putting his hand over the receiver.

"And Dash got his homework done?" asked Helen.

Bob glanced toward the dining room to see Dash sitting at the table, slumped over his math textbook, sleeping. "All done," he lied.

"So things didn't spiral out of control the moment I left?" asked Helen.

"Amazing as it may seem," said Bob, "it has been quite uneventful, in fact. How about you?"

"I SAVED A RUNAWAY TRAIN!" shrieked Helen, happy to finally burst with her exciting news. "It was SO GREAT!" She told Bob every detail of her rescue. He picked up the remote and turned on the television, surfing through the channels. He watched, frowning, as various anchors reported on Elastigirl's big rescue. The story was everywhere.

"I'm on this runaway super train full of passengers

going backward at 200, 250, 300 miles per hour, and I pull this sucker into the station!" she rambled. "BOOM! NO CASUALTIES!" She squealed, delighted. Bob clicked off the television. "I'm telling ya, honey, it was a SAGA!"

"That's fantastic." Bob was really proud of her, but he couldn't deny the fact that he was also very jealous. He missed doing hero work . . . and having all the reporters talk about *his* great rescues. "I'm so proud of you," he said as he banged his head against a wall.

"I'm proud of *you*, honey," said Helen. "I know you want to get out there, and you will—soon. And you'll be amazing. I couldn't have done this if you hadn't taken over so well. Thanks for handling everything."

They said good night, and Bob hung up the phone. He looked at Dash slumbering at the table, then at Jack-Jack, who was now fast asleep, leaning against the sliding-glass door. He gently picked up both boys and carried them upstairs to their bedrooms. Then Bob went to bed.

Even though he was completely exhausted, he tossed and turned. "*'Eh, Dad, it's okay,'*" he grumbled, repeating Dash's words. "*'I'll just wait for Mom to get back'*—as if only *she* could do it. *I* know how to do math," Bob said to himself. He checked the clock. It was a little after two a.m. He sighed, sat up, and headed downstairs, determined to tackle the challenge. "*'Wait for Mom.'* What am I? A substitute parent?"

A few minutes later, he was in the kitchen. He poured himself a cup of coffee and sat at the kitchen table with Dash's math book in front of him. He put on his glasses and began to read.

Dash was sound asleep when Bob gently woke him a few hours later. "I think I understand your math assignment," he whispered. Dash tossed the sheets over his head and groaned. "We still have some time to finish it before your test."

Moments later, Bob, with a big cup of coffee, and Dash, with a glass of juice, sat at the kitchen table going over the math assignment, problem by problem. As Bob explained, Dash nodded, scribbling with his pencil, working to solve the equations.

"You got it?" Bob asked after he was done.

Dash smiled.

"Yeah, baby!" cheered Bob. They clinked glasses, and Bob sent Dash to get dressed for school. With a big grin, he closed the math book and put it into Dash's backpack. "*'Wait for Mom.'*" He chuckled to himself.

9

While Bob was getting Violet and Dash off for another day of school, the Deavors and Elastigirl headed to the KQRY television studio for Elastigirl's interview with news anchor Chad Brentley. They sat in the greenroom watching Chad's live interview with a foreign ambassador. A makeup artist powdered Elastigirl's face, preparing her for the camera. Elastigirl admitted she was a bit nervous. It had been a long time since she was last interviewed. Deavor tried to boost her confidence with a few positive words before a stagehand appeared.

"Ms. Elastigirl? They're ready for you."

Winston and Evelyn wished her luck, and Elastigirl followed the stagehand into the hallway. As they walked toward the set, the ambassador, flanked by her security team, approached.

"Oh!" said Elastigirl. "Madam Ambassador, hello!" She was about to introduce herself when the ambassador pushed past her guards to shake Elastigirl's hand.

"You are Elastigirl!" the ambassador said. She looked tickled to see her. "It was so sad when you went underground, and I am glad to see you are back in your shiny outfit!"

"That means so much coming from you," said Elastigirl. "Good luck with your speech! Bring . . . lasting peace!"

As the ambassador's guards started leading her away, she called, "I will—when you defeat evil!"

Moments later, Elastigirl was sitting next to Chad on the set. She smiled as he introduced her.

"For over fifteen years, Superheroes have been in hiding, forced into it by a society no longer willing to support them. That may soon be changing, due to a growing movement to bring the Supers back. Here, fresh on the heels of her own heroic save of a runaway train, and sporting a new look, is the Superhero Elastigirl. Welcome!"

"Hello, Chad," said Elastigirl, trying to settle in.

"Well, all the polls are going in your direction," said Chad.

"That's true. Things are good—"

Suddenly, Chad's eyes glazed over and his tone shifted as he interrupted Elastigirl. "Hello," he said.

"Uh . . . hello," said Elastigirl, a little confused.

"Do I have your attention?" asked Chad in a robotic voice.

Elastigirl looked at her interviewer, trying to read his face, and noticed a strange flashing-light pattern reflected in his eyes.

"Of course I do," said Chad mechanically. "I'm appearing on your screen. Reading the words I'm saying off another screen."

Elastigirl followed his gaze to the teleprompter, where she caught a glimpse of hypnotic light patterns blazing across the screen. She started to fall under its spell, but averted her eyes just in time, breaking free.

"Screens are everywhere," Chad continued. "We are controlled by screens."

Elastigirl hurried into the studio's control room, where she saw everyone there frozen, transfixed by the dazzling lights flashing across all the screens.

The Screenslaver appeared on the monitors. He wore big, round goggles over a large hood that covered his face. "And screens are controlled by me. The Screenslaver," he added.

Elastigirl yelled at the crew, but they stayed absolutely still, mesmerized by their screens.

"I control this broadcast, and this idiotic anchorman you see before you," continued Chad.

Evelyn hurried over to Elastigirl. "The signal's been hijacked!" she yelled. "I'll check it out!"

Elastigirl ran back to the set and rushed to Chad, trying to slap him out of his trance.

"I could hijack the ambassador's aerocade while it's still airborne, right, Elastigirl?" Chad asked in his robotic voice.

Elastigirl sprinted off the set and into the hallway. "NEAREST WINDOW! WHERE'S THE NEAREST WINDOW?" she shouted. A frightened assistant gestured toward a door, and Elastigirl dashed through it. Spotting a window at the end of another hallway, Elastigirl grabbed a chair and flung it, shattering the glass. She stretched and propelled herself out the window.

Chad's trance seemed to break as he blinked and stared at the camera, bewildered. In the control room, the pulsing lights stopped and the crew snapped out of their trances, too. They looked at their screens and saw Chad looking at the empty chair where Elastigirl had been sitting, wondering where she had gone.

Elastigirl stretched upward, using the buildings to pull herself to a high rooftop. She scanned the horizon and spotted three helicopters in the distance. Then she stretched herself across two buildings, grabbing onto each one, creating a giant slingshot with her body. She aimed for one of the helicopters, pulled herself all the way back, and released, shooting into the sky! The force of it smashed her right through the window of the chopper and she tumbled inside . . . but the ambassador wasn't there.

Elastigirl hurried into the cockpit, and the pilot yelled, "This is a restricted aircraft!"

"Too late!" she yelled back. "They've been compromised!" She told the pilot the ambassador was in danger and asked him which chopper she was in. Suddenly, a helicopter blade sliced through the cockpit, barely missing their heads! Elastigirl figured the ambassador must be in that one, and told the pilot to get her close to it. "Get to safety!" she added. "I'll find the ambassador. And don't look at the screens!"

The pilot flew as close as possible and Elastigirl leaped out, swinging to the other helicopter's window. She pulled herself through as a bullet flew by, just missing her! A security guard held a gun, with the terrified ambassador at his side.

"Stand down!" insisted the ambassador. "It's Elastigirl!"

The guard lowered his gun, and Elastigirl entered the cabin. Turning to the ambassador, she said, "Stay in your seat, ma'am!" Then she tried to open the door to the cockpit, but it was locked. She stretched to grab the security guard's gun and shot the lock off, opening it. Inside were two hypnotized pilots, sitting rigidly at the controls. She quickly punched the screens to break them, releasing the pilots from their trance. They looked completely confused, but there was no time to explain. Elastigirl spotted the third chopper coming straight for them. "GET DOWN!" she shouted.

The helicopter crashed into them, and they careened toward a building! Elastigirl grabbed the controls and pulled up, barely missing it. "Open the door!" she yelled, struggling to gain control of the chopper.

"Do as she says!" the ambassador cried.

The cockpit door opened, and Elastigirl yelled to the pilots, "Can you guys swim?" They both nodded, and Elastigirl stretched a leg back, kicking them out of the helicopter and into the river below. Then she turned to the ambassador. "We're too low to parachute! We're gonna have to slingshot. Hang on! Trust me!"

"I trust you!" shouted the ambassador.

Holding on to the ambassador, Elastigirl stretched herself and snapped back to propel the two of them toward the clouds. Once they were high enough, she flattened and expanded her body, turning into a giant parachute. They gently drifted down to the ground.

"Are you all right, ma'am?" asked Elastigirl.

"I'm fine," said the ambassador. Then she fainted in Elastigirl's arms.

10

The morning after Elastigirl's daring rescue, Dash and Jack-Jack were busy eating breakfast. Bob prepared a plate for Violet as he heard her coming down the stairs.

Violet felt awful. The day before at school, she had asked Tony why he had missed their date, but he acted like she was a complete stranger.

"Boys are jerks, and Superheroes suck," she said, collapsing into her chair.

"Good morning!" said Bob, handing her a plate of waffles.

"He takes one look at me in that suit and decides to pretend he doesn't even know me," Violet said.

"Well, he's protecting himself," said Bob, pouring her some orange juice. "If he really did see you, it's best that he forget." He headed over to the refrigerator and opened the door, placing the juice back inside. "I can't tell you how many memories Dicker's had to erase over the years, when"—Bob pulled out the milk container and sniffed it, assessing whether it was still okay to drink—"someone figured out your mother's or my identity." He closed the refrigerator door and was surprised to see Violet standing right in front of him.

"It was Dicker!" she growled, seething. "You told him about Tony!"

"Honey—" started Bob, feeling guilty.

"You had me erased from Tony's mind!" she yelled.

Violet stomped off. Jack-Jack watched her go, looked at Bob, and dumped his bowl of cereal over his head, laughing. Bob cleaned the cereal from the floor as Violet returned, holding her Supersuit.

"I HATE Superheroes, and I renounce them!" she shouted. Then she marched over to the kitchen sink and stuffed the suit into the garbage disposal. She turned the disposal on and the suit spun around and around—but stayed completely undamaged. Furious, Violet bit into the suit and pulled at it, trying to rip it apart. The suit was indestructible. Bob and Dash watched as Violet finally let out a frustrated shriek, threw the suit against the wall, and stomped off again.

Dash looked at Bob. "Is she having adolescence?" he asked.

Bob sighed in the affirmative and hung his head.

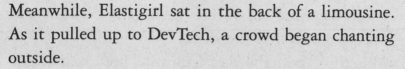

Meanwhile, Elastigirl sat in the back of a limousine. As it pulled up to DevTech, a crowd began chanting outside.

"KABOOM! KAPOW! SUPERS SHOULD BE LEGAL NOW!"

Elastigirl asked the driver what was going on.

"They're here in support," he replied.

"Support of what?" she asked.

"Well, in support of you."

Elastigirl exited the car, and a cheer erupted as the adoring crowd reached out, trying to shake her hand. She couldn't believe she had inspired so many people.

"Thanks for coming!" she said. She crouched down to shake a little girl's hand and noticed her sign. It read THE SCREENSLAVER IS STILL OUT THERE. Suddenly, all the joy she felt from the outpouring of admiration disappeared. She knew it was true. She still had a villain to catch.

Elastigirl entered Winston's office to find him busy answering calls. He handed her one of the newspapers scattered across his desk, pointing out a headline: SAVED AMBASSADOR GIVES PRO-SUPER SPEECH.

"It's working!" he said. He told Elastigirl that he was getting calls from all over the world. Then he told her about the next phase. "We're going to have a summit at sea! We'll use our yacht! We'll gather leaders and Supers from all over the world. . . ."

Elastigirl said she was happy to hear it, but she sounded pretty glum. When Winston asked her what was wrong, she said she was upset that she hadn't caught the Screenslaver.

He told her she should take time to appreciate the victories. "What do you want on your tombstone? 'She worried a lot'?" he asked.

"All right, stop talking," said Evelyn. "Show her."

Winston smiled and nodded. Then he led Elastigirl into a room full of Supers. She didn't recognize any of them, but they were all wearing Supersuits, many of which looked homemade. When she entered, they erupted in excitement, applauding and looking at her with great respect.

One woman rushed up and awkwardly introduced herself. "I—my Superhero name is Voyd. I just want to thank you for, like, for being you, and . . . I just, like . . . Okay, what I can do, um, is this. . . ." Blushing, the woman grabbed a mug from a table. She flung it into the air, and as it dropped, she used her Super power to create a series of portals. The mug fell in and out of them as Voyd continued to show off her special skill. Finally, the mug fell out of the last portal and landed back on the desk where it had started. There was a moment of silence as everyone in the room took in what they'd just seen. Then they broke out in applause.

"That's fantastic," said Elastigirl.

"I felt like an outcast," said Voyd. "Before. But now, with you being . . . you, I feel like . . ." Too emotional to finish her sentence, Voyd hugged Elastigirl. "Yay, me," she added.

Elastigirl was truly touched.

"I flew them in from all over," said Winston. "They've all been in hiding. They have powers, secret identities, and names they've given themselves."

The Supers were ecstatic to meet Elastigirl and share their stories.

"I'm Screech," said one Super, who resembled an owl. "I've always considered you the gold standard for Superheroes."

"Well, thanks!" said Elastigirl, flattered. "You're too nice!"

"I am called Brick," said a large woman with a serious expression. Elastigirl asked her where she was from, and she answered, "Wisconsin."

Another Super named He-lectrix explained his powers. "You know, zapping things electronically, charging things, bolts of lightning, that kinda stuff."

An older man approached. "Name's Reflux," he said. "Medical condition or Super power? You decide. . . ." He laughed, and Elastigirl chuckled along with him. "That's a little line I say just to put people at ease. Hope I don't offend."

"Oh, no no no, that's fantastic," Elastigirl said.

The Supers hung out, chatting away as the time flew by. Elastigirl couldn't believe what a positive impact she had made on these people. She felt proud of her decision to take the job to make Supers legal again, and that felt great.

Once the party started winding down and Winston bid everyone a good night, Elastigirl and Evelyn sat down together for a drink.

"It must be nice for you. Being out front after all this time," said Evelyn.

"Out front?" asked Elastigirl.

"Well, it's been a while since your Superhero days.

And even then, you were kind of in Mr. Incredible's shadow," said Evelyn.

Elastigirl smiled. "Oh, I beg to differ," she replied. Then she asked Evelyn how she felt about her brother running DevTech.

"I don't want his job. I invent; he sells," said Evelyn.

The two continued to chat until an idea popped into Elastigirl's mind. She knew how to capture the Screenslaver! "I need to lock onto a signal and trace its origin."

Elastigirl and Evelyn worked out the details. Evelyn would create a tracking device. Then they would schedule a remote interview with Chad Brentley and set a trap for the Screenslaver.

The two women bumped fists, more than ready to carry out their plan.

11

Back at home, Bob picked up the phone and dialed as he unpacked a few moving boxes. Dicker answered, and Bob asked him if he remembered wiping Tony's mind.

"Yeah," said Dicker. "Nice kid."

"Well, you also wiped out the Friday-night date my daughter had with him. In fact, you wiped out my daughter," Bob said.

"Oops. Not an exact science, Bob," said Dicker.

"Rick, you gotta help me here," said Bob. "Violet hates me. And you. And Superheroes. I gotta fix this. What do you know about Tony?"

Dicker had already moved to his filing cabinet and was thumbing through the files. He found Tony's. He opened it and quickly scanned it. "Not much. Seems like a good kid. Popular. Plays sports. Music. Parents own the Happy Platter. Kid works there part-time."

"Happy . . . Platter . . . ?" said Bob, concocting an idea. He thanked Dicker for his time and hung up the phone, turning his attention back to unpacking.

Later that evening, Bob gathered the kids and took them out to the Happy Platter restaurant. It was a modest place with wood paneling and linoleum floors.

Violet looked around, a bit confused. "Why did we drive all the way across town for the Happy Platter?" asked Violet.

Bob faced the hostess. "We'd like a booth over there, near the philodendron," he said, ignoring Violet's question.

The hostess nodded unenthusiastically, grabbed some menus, and led them toward the booth.

As they followed her, Violet added, "This platter doesn't look all that happy to me. It looks . . . bored,"

"Ha! The Bored Platter," said Dash.

"I thought Vi would want a change of pace from drive-in food," said Bob.

"I like drive-in food," said Violet.

"Does this mean vegetables?" asked Dash.

"A balanced diet means vegetables, kiddo. Get used to it," said Bob.

Their server arrived with a pitcher of water and began pouring it into red plastic tumblers. Violet took a sip as the server said, "Good evening, everyone." She looked up and gagged, water spurting out of her nose. It was Tony Rydinger!

"Whoa! Hey, Violet, are you okay?" asked Bob.

"EWWW!" exclaimed Dash.

"Is she all right?" asked Tony. He handed her some napkins and tried to make her feel less embarrassed by saying, "It's okay, it's fine, happens all the time."

"I'm okay. I'm fine," said Violet, wishing she could use her invisibility power and disappear.

Bob asked for more napkins.

"Maybe she needs something bigger," said Dash. "Like a towel."

Tony pulled a wad of napkins from his pocket, and he and Bob helped mop up the water. Violet lowered her head, letting her hair fall around her face, trying to hide as she continued to cough.

"Normally she doesn't ever drip like this," said Bob.

Tony looked at Bob. "Would, uhh . . . would you like water, sir?"

Violet coughed and coughed as Tony filled Bob's glass to the top.

"This is my daughter," said Bob. "Who you must know, right?"

"God. Stop," said Violet under her breath.

"Hello," said Tony, facing Violet.

"Violet . . ."

"Hello, Violet," said Tony.

"Hey, Vi, say hi to—"

"Don't push it, Dad," Violet said, interrupting him through gritted teeth.

"I'm Dash, her little brother." Dash reached over and shook Tony's hand.

"This is really good water," said Bob enthusiastically. "It's very refreshing. Spring water, is it?"

"I don't know, sir. I think it's tap," said Tony.

"Well, it is very good," repeated Bob.

"Excellent tap," said Dash, raising his glass to Tony.

Unable to handle another mortifying second, Violet excused herself, got up from the table, and walked away.

Tony smiled at Bob, Dash, and Jack-Jack. "Nice to meet you," he said. Then he walked off.

"Well, where'd SHE go?" asked Bob.

"To find a good place to be angry?" said Dash.

12

Inside the KQRY television studio, Chad Brentley introduced his special remote interview with Elastigirl.

"How you feeling, Chad?" asked Elastigirl, her voice coming through a speaker.

"I'm fine—the doctors checked me out," he said. "I have NO memory of the event. I gotta tell you, it's pretty strange to see a recording of yourself from the night before and have no recollection." Chad then told the viewers that the studio had taken additional precautions to prevent the Screenslaver from attacking again. Continuing with the interview, he asked Elastigirl where she was.

"On a case," she said. "In a secure undisclosed location." Unbeknownst to Chad, Elastigirl sat directly on top of the studio, on a large transmission tower. She watched the news show on her handheld device.

Chad showed a clip taken from Elastigirl's suit cam during the hovertrain rescue. Viewers watched from her point of view as she sprang into action, jumping onto her Elasticycle and taking off after the train. Then the footage suddenly became fuzzy as the newscast turned to static and the Screenslaver appeared!

"The Screenslaver interrupts this program for an important announcement," he said. His voice sounded deep and warped, as if it had been electronically altered.

Elastigirl studied the screen of her handheld tracker as it worked to locate the source of the Screenslaver's transmission. Once it was locked in, Elastigirl looked in the direction of the signal and whispered, "Gotcha."

Inside DevTech, the Deavors both watched with anticipation. "I'll be—" said Evelyn. "She knew. . . ."

"Let's see if your gadget works," said Winston.

Elastigirl continued to check the tracker as she followed it toward the Screenslaver's location. She stretched across rooftops and vaulted herself from one building to the next as she followed the signal.

"Don't bother watching the rest," said the Screenslaver, still on the screen. "Elastigirl doesn't save the day; she only postpones her defeat." He went on to rant about how people use screens because they're lazy. And how they want Superheroes to take care of them so they don't have to take care of themselves. "Go ahead, send your Supers to stop me. Grab your snacks, watch your screen, and see what happens. You are no longer in control. I am."

Elastigirl fired herself like a slingshot to the top of a building in a dark part of the city. Thousands of antennae jutted out of the rooftops, messing with her signal, but luckily, she was close to her destination. She followed the tracker to the side of an apartment building and faced a window covered in thick wrought iron bars.

Flattening herself, she slipped through the bars and got into the building. She hurried along a hallway and approached the apartment where the Screenslaver's transmission was coming from.

Stretching out her arm, she snaked it beneath the door and unlocked it. The apartment looked like a messy laboratory with tools, lenses, and masks strewn about. Elastigirl walked through it, inspecting all the stuff scattered around: plans for the hovertrain, sketches of helicopters, scientific textbooks, and tattered notebooks. Then she noticed a piece of fabric covering something on a table. She walked toward it and lifted it to reveal a pair of goggles strapped to a mannequin head.

"Find anything interesting?" a voice asked. The Screenslaver appeared behind her with an electronic tool. He slammed the door, locking them both in a large wire cage, and zapped her with his Taser! Then he flicked on hypnotic lights that were scattered on the cage walls. The bright lights blinked and swirled in a mesmerizing pattern. Elastigirl tried to shield her eyes, but he zapped her again. She fought back hard and managed to push him out of the cage.

They continued battling inside the apartment, crashing into bookshelves and furniture, until finally, the Screenslaver escaped through the door, activating a timer on his way out.

As Elastigirl took off after him, the Screenslaver yanked on one of the building's fire alarms and it let out a blaring sound. Ceiling sprinklers rained down as people ran out of their apartments, creating chaos around the chase. Just as she was about to reach the Screenslaver, he slid down an elevator shaft and onto a roof. Then he leaped off the building! But Elastigirl was right behind him. She stretched herself into a parachute, grabbed the Screenslaver in midair, and floated down with him. As she did, the timer went off and the apartment building exploded behind them! They landed and Elastigirl ripped off his mask.

"Elastigirl?" he said, confused. "Wh-what happened?"

"What happened is you destroyed my evidence," she said, irritated, looking over at the leveled apartment building.

Moments later, Elastigirl watched as the cops took the Screenslaver away in handcuffs. "What's going on?" he asked, sounding puzzled.

"That's right, punk. Blame the system," said the cop.

Elastigirl pulled her emblem away from her chest, looking down at the suit cam. "Your tracker worked like a charm," she said, knowing Evelyn was watching. "You're a genius."

"Aw, shucks," said Evelyn, chuckling. "I'm just the genius behind the genius."

They both smiled, feeling great—their plan had worked!

13

In the Parr house, Bob looked dazed as he watched TV with Jack-Jack. Suddenly, Dash burst in.

"Hey, Dad," he said, holding up his math textbook. "We're doing fractions and demicels and percentages, and I don't get 'em."

Bob rubbed his eyes. "Didn't we get all caught up?"

"Yeah, we WERE caught up, and now we're doing fractions and percentages and demicels."

"Decimals," Bob said.

A news story flashed on the television, catching Bob's attention. A reporter announced, "Superheroes are back in the news again, and so is their gear. The car collection of billionaire Victor Cachet grew a little bit more SUPER today with the addition of the INCREDIBILE, the Super car once driven by Superhero Mr. Incredible."

"It's the kind of thing you buy when you have everything else," said the smug billionaire, standing beside the gleaming Incredibile.

"They said it was beyond repair," said Bob, staring at the television.

"And hey, it was in perfect condition," added the billionaire, tapping the hood of the amazing vehicle.

"You used to drive THAT?" asked Dash.

"They said it was destroyed," said Bob, his anger growing by the second.

"Long thought lost or destroyed, the famous car turned up at a private auction," said the reporter.

"They said it was— THAT'S MY CAR!" yelled Bob, finally releasing his fury. He bolted from the room.

SPLASH! Bob fell into one of the hidden rivers in the floor of the house. Grumbling, he pulled himself out of the water and marched into the den. Soaking wet, he began rummaging through some boxes until he finally found what he was looking for: the remote control to the Incredibile!

Bob ran back to the television with Dash on his heels.

The reporter turned to the Incredibile's new owner.

"This car's just *loaded* with amazing gadgets. Care to demonstrate?"

Victor Cachet smiled. "I'd love to, but we haven't figured out how to make them work yet."

Bob pressed the remote and the Incredibile roared to life! The reporter and Victor looked at the car, both stunned as it spun around and around.

"WOW!" said Dash. "IT WORKS?"

Dash snatched the remote from Bob and pressed a button. On the screen, people dove out of the way as dual rocket launchers emerged from the car's grill.

"WHAT ARE YOU DOING?" said Bob, retrieving the remote. He pressed another button and the rocket launchers retracted.

"THIS IS NOT A TOY!" yelled Bob. "That's a rocket launcher!"

"Sweeeet!" said Dash, snatching back the remote. "Which one launches the rockets?"

"HEY! This is not your car!"

"It's not your car either!" said Dash, gesturing to the television.

"It is SO! It's the Incredibile!"

"Well, why's that guy have it?" asked Dash.

"Well, he SHOULDN'T!" Bob said. He grabbed the remote back and pressed another button. The rocket launchers reappeared. Dash tried to grab the remote, but Bob kept it from him.

"Launch the rockets!" chanted Dash.

"I'm not launching anything!" said Bob. "Do you think I want an angry rich guy coming after me right now? When I'm trying not to . . . distract . . . your . . . mother?"

Everyone on the news show had taken cover from the suddenly dangerous car. Bob grunted as he pressed the remote again, powering down the Incredibile.

"So . . . you're not gonna blow up the rich guy's wall?" asked Dash.

Bob sank into the sofa next to Jack-Jack. *ACHOO!* Jack-Jack sneezed and suddenly flew across the room and up the stairs with a jet of smoke coming out of his nose and mouth! Intangible as a ghost, he disappeared through the wall, leaving a smoldering ring of fire.

"*AHHHH!*" Upstairs in her room, Violet screamed. Jack-Jack sneezed again and Violet appeared, running from Jack-Jack, who was now a little red monster!

"What the heck is that?" shrieked Violet.

Jack-Jack smiled, showing off his fangs. Then he transformed back into his normal baby self.

"Jack-Jack has . . . powers?" asked Dash, completely shocked.

"Well—yeah—but, um," Bob stammered as he nodded his head.

"You knew about this?" asked Violet. She couldn't believe he hadn't told them. She asked him if he had told their mother.

Bob put Jack-Jack into his playpen and answered nervously, "Yeah. I dunno—NO. Your mother is not—because I didn't want—because it's not the time—because—"

"Why not?" asked Violet, shocked. "Why would you not tell Mom?"

Dash, finally processing the information, added, "We're your kids! We need to know these things! You'd want us to tell YOU, wouldn't you!" Then he quietly added, "Come on, man. So uncool."

Violet still wanted him to answer her question: Why hadn't he told their mother? "What! Why?"

"Because I'm FORMULATING, OKAY!" Bob yelled. His intensity forced Violet and Dash to jump back. The kids watched as Bob exploded into a rant, venting all his feelings. "I'M TAKING IN INFORMATION! I'M PROCESSING! I'M DOING THE MATH, I'M FIXING THE BOYFRIEND AND KEEPING THE BABY FROM TURNING INTO A FLAMING MONSTER! HOW DO I DO

IT? BY ROLLING WITH THE PUNCHES, BABY! I EAT THUNDER AND CRAP LIGHTNING, OKAY? BECAUSE I'M MR. INCREDIBLE! NOT 'MR. SO-SO' OR 'MR. MEDIOCRE GUY'! MR. INCREDIBLE!"

There was a short moment of silence as Violet and Dash waited, to be sure he was finished. They looked at each other, and Violet said, "We should call Lucius."

"NO," said Bob. "I can handle it! There's no way I'm gonna—" Bob screamed as Jack-Jack hiccupped and burst into flames. Then Jack-Jack sneezed, turned into a smoking ball of fire, and flew right up through the roof of the house!

Bob let out a primal scream as he ran outside and into the backyard. He scrambled as he looked up, trying to get under the baby. He dove to catch him, and they both splashed down into a pool!

Dash and Violet watched Bob emerge from the water holding Jack-Jack, who was now back to his usual self, giggling and cooing.

"I'm calling Lucius," said Violet.

14

A little later, Lucius came to the house. He stood with Bob as they watched Jack-Jack play with his teddy bear in the middle of the family room.

"Looks normal to me," said Lucius. "When did this start happening?"

"Since Helen got the job," said Bob.

"I assume she knows," said Lucius.

"Are you kidding?" said Bob. "I can't tell her about this, not while she's doing hero work!"

Jack-Jack walked over to the television, pointing and calling out, "Mama! Mama!"

Bob saw Elastigirl on the screen. He changed the channel as he and Lucius continued to talk.

"When was the last time you slept?" asked Lucius.

"Who keeps track of that?" said Bob, sounding a

little insane. "Besides, he's a baby. I can handle it, I got this handled—"

"So . . . you good, then?" said Lucius, sarcastically. "You got everything under control, right?"

Just then, Jack-Jack vanished!

Bob rushed to the kitchen and grabbed the cookie jar. "Cha-cha wanna cookie? Num-Num cookie. Cha-cha wanna Num-Num?" said Bob.

Lucius started freaking out because Jack-Jack was gone, but Bob continued to try to tempt the baby back with cookies. Out of nowhere, Jack-Jack reappeared. He took a cookie, gobbled it down, and reached toward Bob for more.

"Whoa," said Lucius. "Okay. So, he can still hear you from—"

"From the other dimension. Yeah," replied Bob, his voice flat.

Lucius had never seen anything like it. "That is freaky. I mean, that's not like—"

"Not like our other kids. No, it is not. Full powers. Totally random," said Bob.

Jack-Jack reached for the cookie jar and said, "Num-Num? Num-Num?"

"So now . . . he's what? Is he good?" asked Lucius.

Bob smiled. "Well, you'd think so, right?" Then

his smile dropped as he looked at Lucius with wild eyes. "Obviously, I can't keep giving him cookies!" Bob sounded more and more unstable as Jack-Jack continued to request cookies. "But if I stop—" Bob closed the cookie jar to demonstrate.

Jack-Jack started getting angry. "NUM-NUM!" he demanded.

With a quick *POP*, Jack-Jack transformed into the red monster and gnawed up and down Bob's arm.

"HE IS FREAKIN'!" said Lucius, in a panic.

"No!" said Bob, trying to get the monster baby off his arm. "No biting the daddy! No biting!"

Later, Bob and Lucius were slumped on the couch, staring off into space. Jack-Jack sat between them snacking on something. Once it was gone, he looked down at his empty hands and then over at Lucius, frowning and babbling angrily. Lucius conjured a smooth ball of ice and gave it to him. Jack-Jack happily gummed it.

"I think I just need a little bit of 'me' time," said Bob, his voice cracking. "Then I'll be good to go."

"Oh, you need more than 'me' time, Bob," said Lucius. "You need major life realignment on a number of levels. Starting with baby super freak here. You need some solid, outside-the-box thinking."

Bob thought about what Lucius had said, and later that day, he headed out with Jack-Jack. He soon pulled the car up to an ornate front gate, and Edna Mode's eyes appeared on the security monitor.

"Galbaki?" shouted Edna. Her face filled the screen. "Elastigirl's Supersuit is by Galbaki! Explain yourself!"

Bob stared into the monitor, too worn out to speak.

"Oh my God, you're worse than I thought," said Edna, narrowing her eyes at him disapprovingly.

"It's the baby," Bob said. "I brought the baby." He leaned back, revealing Jack-Jack in his car seat making loud screeching sounds.

"Highly unusual," said Edna.

The laser gate opened and Bob drove through.

Moments later, Bob carried Jack-Jack as he walked beside Edna toward her entrance hall.

"You look ghastly, Robert," said Edna, leading him into her gigantic living room.

"I haven't been sleeping. . . . I broke my daughter. . . . They keep changing math . . . ," he rambled. "We needed double-A batteries, but I got triple-As, and now we still need double-A batteries; I put one red thing in with a load of whites and now everything's pink. And I think we need eggs."

Edna shook her head. "Done properly, parenting is a heroic act. Done properly," she repeated. "I am fortunate that it has never afflicted me. But you do not come to me for eggs and batteries, Robert. I design herowear . . . and Elastigirl must have a new suit."

Bob collapsed into a chair and placed Jack-Jack on the floor. "Actually, it's Jack-Jack," he said.

Jack-Jack toddled toward Edna.

"You also wish for a new suit for the baby?" she asked, backing away from him. "I would hardly classify this as an emergency. . . ."

"Well, he's a special case," said Bob. "Worth studying. If I could just leave him with you for a while, I—"

"Leave him? HERE?" said Edna, cutting him off. She looked down at Jack-Jack, irritated as he grabbed the edge of her robe and stuffed it into his mouth. She quickly snatched it from him. "I am not a baby person, Robert! I have no baby facilities! I am an artist; I do not involve myself in the prosaic day-to-day."

Jack-Jack gazed at Edna intensely. Suddenly, his nose inflated and looked identical to hers. Edna's voice drifted off as she became absorbed in Jack-Jack's slow transformation. Feature by feature, he began to turn into Edna—right down to the short black hair.

"Fascinating," said Edna. "Are you seeing this, Robert?" She glanced over at Bob, who seemed to be sleeping with his eyes still open. Edna turned back to Jack-Jack, who sneezed, rocketing up toward the high ceiling. As he plummeted down, Edna dove to catch him. But he sneezed again and stopped, midair, and returned to his original Jack-Jack form. He hovered above Edna's outstretched hands and giggled.

"Oh my God . . . YES," said Edna.

Edna carried Jack-Jack in one arm while shooing Bob out with the other. "Of course you can leave the baby overnight," she said, rapidly firing out the words. "I'm sure filling in for Helen is challenging and you are very tired, and the other children need you and miss you and you must go to them. Auntie Edna will take care of everything." She cooed at Jack-Jack and impatiently ushered Bob out the door. "So drive safely and goodbye. I enjoy our visits."

Bob stood at the doorstep, a little confused. "Auntie Edna?" he said to himself.

THE INCREDIBLES

JACK-JACK

MR. INCREDIBLE

ELASTIGIRL

VIOLET

DASH

	ROBERT PARR	HELEN PARR	VIOLET PARR	DASHIELL PARR	JACK-JACK PARR
ALIAS					
ABILITIES	SUPER STRENGTH	FULL-BODY ELASTICITY	INVISIBILITY AND FORCE-FIELD GENERATION	SUPER SPEED	TELEKINESIS, MIMICRY, DIMENSIONAL TELEPORTATION, SPONTANEOUS COMBUSTION, LEVITATION, SELF-CLONING, MONSTROUS TENDENCIES
WEAKNESSES	BIG EGO	FREEZING TEMPERATURES	INEXPERIENCE	IMPULSE CONTROL	UNKNOWN

OTES: The Incredibles prove that the only thing stronger than a Super is a family of Supers!

FROZONE

ALIAS

LUCIUS BEST

ABILITIES

► CAN GENERATE ICE FROM MOISTURE IN THE AIR
► MASTER SPEED SKATER ON ICE PATHWAYS THAT HE CREATES

WEAKNESSES

► REQUIRES MOISTURE TO CREATE ICE

NOTES: In addition to his amazing freezing powers, Frozone has his own clothing line and music label.

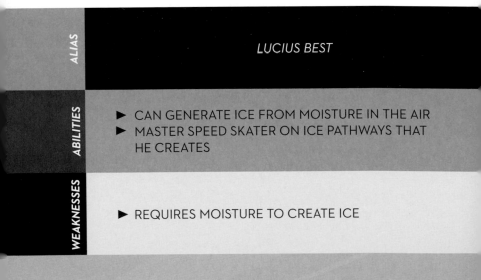

VOYD

ALIAS	*KAREN (LAST NAME UNKNOWN)*
ABILITIES	▶ DIMENSIONAL TELEPORTATION
WEAKNESSES	▶ WORMHOLE DESTINATIONS CAN BE UNPREDICTABLE

NOTES: Voyd's ability to generate wormholes makes her a formidable hero and perfect for missions that require long-distance travel and quick escapes.

HE-LECTRIX

ALIAS

UNKNOWN

ABILITIES

► ABILITY TO CONTROL AND PROJECT ELECTRICAL CURRENTS
► IMPERVIOUS TO ELECTRICITY

WEAKNESSES

► EXPOSURE TO WATER CAN TEMPORARILY SHORT OUT HE-LECTRIX'S POWER. ALSO, HIS POWERS HAVE NO EFFECT ON NONCONDUCTIVE MATERIALS.

NOTES: Villains who encounter this high-voltage hero are in for the shock of their lives!

BRICK

ALIAS

CONCRETIA "CONNIE" MASON

ABILITIES

► CAN EXPAND TO THE SIZE AND STRENGTH OF A BRICK WALL ON COMMAND

WEAKNESSES

► WILL SINK IN WATER

NOTES: When Brick arrives, evildoers find themselves between a rock and a hard place.

REFLUX

ALIAS

GUS BURNS

ABILITIES

► CAN REGURGITATE HIS MOLTEN STOMACH ACID

WEAKNESSES

► TIRES EASILY AND OVERHEATS
► MOTION SICKNESS

NOTES: When Reflux goes on the offensive, he is *the* most offensive hero around.

SCREECH

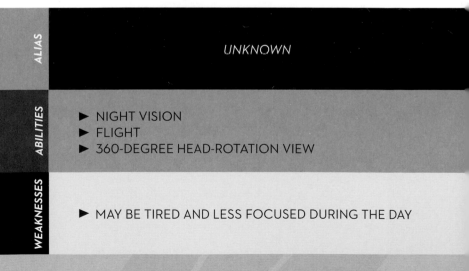

ALIAS

UNKNOWN

ABILITIES

► NIGHT VISION
► FLIGHT
► 360-DEGREE HEAD-ROTATION VIEW

WEAKNESSES

► MAY BE TIRED AND LESS FOCUSED DURING THE DAY

NOTES: Screech's ability to fly is natural and not a function of his suit, which serves to enhance his owl-like features.

KRUSHAUER

ALIAS

UNKNOWN

ABILITIES

► CAN CRUSH OBJECTS WITHOUT TOUCHING THEM

WEAKNESSES

► CAN ONLY CRUSH INANIMATE OBJECTS

NOTES: When Krushauer battles the bad guys, he never fails to leave a lasting impression and a trail of rubble in his wake.

A little later, Violet looked up as Bob entered the house without the baby. "Where's Jack-Jack?" she asked.

"E's taking him for a little bit," he said.

"Edna is . . . *babysitting*?" she asked, shocked.

"Yeah."

"And you're okay with this?" asked Violet, wondering what she was missing.

Bob looked more tired than ever, but he grinned widely as he crossed to the couch and collapsed onto it. "Yeah," he said with a heavy sigh. "I don't know why, but yeah." He took a deep breath. "I wanted to say something to you." He stared out at the wall. "I'm sorry about Tony. I didn't think about Dicker erasing his memory, or about you having to pay the price for a choice you never made. It's not fair, I know. And then I made it worse at the restaurant by trying to—" He stopped himself, realizing he was rambling. He sighed before continuing. "Anyway, I'm sorry. I'm used to knowing what the right thing to do is, but now I'm not sure anymore. I just want to be a good dad."

Violet smiled. "You're not good"—she wrapped her arms around him and gave him a hug—"you're Super."

Bob began to snore, and Violet realized that even though he was sitting straight up, he was fast asleep.

15

The Deavors' penthouse was lavishly decorated, as a party was in full swing. Live music played, and both Supers and non-Supers enjoyed chatting, eating, and drinking. Giant video screens on the walls displayed a slow-motion loop of Elastigirl's suit-cam footage that showed her capture of the Screenslaver. Crowds of people circled around Elastigirl as they celebrated her success.

Winston Deavor called everyone's attention as he raised his champagne glass. "I want to thank everyone who came out tonight in support of Superheroes and bringing them back to society." The crowd applauded. "You all made it happen! The need for this has been made crystal clear in recent days, with bad actors like the self-proclaimed Screenslaver threatening our peace. His reign was short, huh?" He held up the

Screenslaver's mask and hood, and the crowd roared with approval. "And thanks to this woman . . . a great Super, you love her, you missed her . . . WELCOME BACK, ELASTIGIRL! Come on up here—don't be bashful!"

The crowd applauded as Elastigirl reluctantly made her way to the microphone. Winston hugged her and handed her the Screenslaver headgear. "I want you to have this. A memento," he whispered.

"Thanks, Winston, Evelyn, and everyone at DevTech," said Elastigirl. "I am forever in your debt. And thanks to *all* of you. Your pressure changed the right minds!"

She handed the microphone back to Winston and he made another announcement. "Just now at a worldwide summit, leaders from more than a hundred of the world's top countries have agreed to make Superheroes legal again!" Enthusiastic cheers filled the room. "We'll gather Superheroes and leaders from all over the planet on our ship, the *EVERJUST,* for a televised signing ceremony at sea!"

The live music started up again, and everyone continued to enjoy the celebration. As a swarm of Supers ran up to congratulate Elastigirl, her eyes drifted to one of the monitors playing the Screenslaver loop. She fixated on his face and just knew, deep in her gut, that something was not right.

Later that evening, as the party started winding down, Elastigirl slipped away to the editing suite. She began to review some of the raw footage of the Screenslaver captured by her suit cam.

Just then, Evelyn entered, carrying drinks. "Are Superheroes allowed?" she asked, offering Elastigirl one.

"I am definitely not on duty," said Elastigirl. "Ignore the costume."

She smiled as Evelyn handed her a drink. They clinked glasses.

"Had to step away from the grips 'n' grins, you know?" said Elastigirl.

"Gotta get away to keep it pure," said Evelyn. "I know I do."

"Get away . . . from what?"

"Eh, you know, company stuff. My brother, mostly."

"But you love him. You two *are* this company—Yin and Yang."

"Yeah, I invent the stuff; he's good with people— pleasing them, engaging them, giving out what they want. I never know what people want."

"What do you think they want?" asked Elastigirl.

"Ease. People will trade quality for ease every time. It may be crap, but it's so convenient."

Elastigirl thought about her words and said, "Yeah. Kinda like this case." She explained that something was not sitting right with her. "It was too easy," she added.

"THAT was too easy? Wow . . . ," said Evelyn.

Elastigirl's eyes drifted back to the screen on the editing machine and she noticed something. "Look at that," she said, pointing to an image. "One of the Screenslaver's monitors is tuned into my suit cam."

"What?" Evelyn looked closer as Elastigirl used the controls to rock the image back and forth.

"Isn't the suit cam a closed circuit?" asked Elastigirl.

"It is," replied Evelyn.

"Then how come the Screenslaver has it?"

"Maybe he—hacked it?"

"So he's sophisticated enough to do that, but he has simple locks on his doors?" said Elastigirl, trying to work out the mystery in her mind.

"Maybe he wanted you to find him," suggested Evelyn.

"He wanted to get caught?" Elastigirl asked, doubtful.

"He wanted you to win," said Evelyn.

Elastigirl frowned. "That makes no sense. He's a brilliant guy. If he's smart enough to conceive of technology like this, he's smart enough to think of something to DO with it. The guy we put in jail delivered pizzas—"

"So? Einstein was a patent clerk. Look. You won. You got the guy who—"

"WAIT," said Elastigirl. Her mind was racing with thoughts. "All the Screenslaver needs to do to hypnotize someone is get a screen in front of their eyes. But what if the screen doesn't look like a screen?" She lifted up the Screenslaver hood and goggles fell out. She picked them up and inspected them closely. "What if the pizza guy is really a pizza guy, but he was controlled by the screens built into his glasses?"

Evelyn's hands flew out and she forced the goggles over Elastigirl's eyes. In an instant, their lenses blazed with light, sending Elastigirl into a hypnotic state.

"You are good," said Evelyn.

16

Bob opened his eyes, in a fog, and looked around the family room. It only took a few seconds for it to dawn on him: he had spent the whole night on the couch. Violet had removed his shoes and given him a blanket and a pillow. Dash sat at the end of the couch, eating a bowl of cereal and watching television.

"I thought it was best to just let you sleep," said Violet. "Seventeen hours. How do you feel?"

Bob grinned. "Super."

Later, at Edna's house, Bob was walking with Edna and Jack-Jack toward her lab. Jack-Jack imitated her step for step.

"I can't tell you how much I appreciate you watching Jack-Jack for me, E," said Bob.

"Yes, I'm sure your gratitude is quite inexpressible," said Edna. "Don't ask me to do it again, *dahling;* my rates are far too high." Bob stuttered in his response, and Edna said, "I'm joking, Robert. I enjoyed the assignment. He is bright and I am stimulating—we deserve each other."

Jack-Jack continued to imitate Edna as they approached the lab.

"Your child is a polymorph," she said. "Like all babies, he has enormous potential. It is not unknown for Supers to have more than one power when young, but this little one has many." She turned to Jack-Jack. "Yes?" she said adoringly. "You have many powers?"

Jack-Jack babbled back to her. When they arrived at the door to the lab, Edna punched a code on the keypad, then picked him up for the security protocol. Like an old pro, Jack-Jack placed his hand on the scanner, opened his eyes wide for the retinal scan, and said into the microphone, "Ba-ba-bow."

Edna grinned at Bob as the doors opened and they entered the lab. "I understand you lack sleep and coherency, Robert," said Edna, directing him to sit in one of the chairs affixed to a moving platform. "Babies can be anything, and your child is no exception! He is pure unlimited potential, Robert! He slept while I worked in a creative fever!" She shifted her voice to address Jack-Jack. "Auntie Edna stayed up all night making sure you look fabulous in your many forms." She placed Jack-Jack in the testing chamber and closed the door.

Bob's eyes went wide. "What're you . . . ? You're putting him in the—?"

"In the chamber, Robert. He is part of the demonstration and will be fine," she said. "Your challenge is to manage a baby who has multiple powers and no control over them, yes?"

"That sums it up," said Bob.

"I often work to music, and I noticed the baby responds well to it, specifically Mozart," said Edna. She pressed a button, and music began to play over the speaker system. Jack-Jack snapped to attention, completely engaged. "I blended Kevlar with carbine for durability under duress and cotton for comfort," she continued. Then she handed him a sleek monitor, its screen full of information. "Interwoven with these fabrics is a mesh of tiny sensors that monitor the baby's physical properties—"

Suddenly, the monitor lit up and read REPLICATION IMMINENT IN 3, 2, 1—

Jack-Jack stood up and fell to the floor. As soon as he hit it, he multiplied into five Jack-Jacks, and they all happily danced around the chamber to the music.

"Oh, lord," Bob said. "What's he doing?"

"Well, it's Mozart, Robert!" said Edna. "Can you blame him? The important thing is that the suit and tracker anticipated the change and alerted you."

She pressed a button, and a cookie appeared in the chamber, mounted to a moving pole. All the Jack-Jacks focused on the cookie and began to chase after it as it moved across the chamber. Just before the Jack-Jacks reached the cookie, it disappeared, vanishing through a door in the chamber. One by one, the Jack-Jacks slapped into the wall and merged back into a single Jack-Jack.

Bob started to panic. "Oh, no," he said. "Cookies! I gotta get cookies!"

"You do not need cookies," said Edna. "As I learned quite painfully last night, any solution involving cookies will inevitably result in the demon baby."

Bob and Edna looked down at the tracker. It read PHASE SHIFT DETECTED. Jack-Jack tried to penetrate the wall but was unable to, and quickly became very angry, turning into the red monster. Then the tracking pad lit up: COMBUSTION IMMINENT.

"What does THAT mean?" asked Bob. Just then, Jack-Jack burst into flames and Bob screamed.

"It means 'fire,' Robert," said Edna. "For which the suit has countermeasures. I suggest you extinguish the baby's flames before he trips the sprinkler system."

Bob hit the tracker, and foam erupted from Jack-Jack's suit, quickly putting out the fire. Jack-Jack giggled, licking the substance from his face.

"The flame retardant is blackberry lavender, *dahling*," said Edna. "Effective, edible, and delicious."

"Well, whaddya know," said Bob with a relieved chuckle. "That is useful."

A little later, Bob clutched Jack-Jack in one arm and an Edna Mode bag in the other while he stood on Edna's doorstep, thanking her for everything. When he asked her how much he owed her, she cut him off.

"Eh, pish-posh, *dahling*. Your bill will be deducted from my fee for being Mr. Incredible's, Elastigirl's, and Frozone's EXCLUSIVE designer throughout the known universe and until the end of time." Edna watched as Bob buckled Jack-Jack into his car seat and added, "But babysitting this one . . . I do for free, *dahling*." She caressed Jack-Jack's cheek and said goodbye.

17

Elastigirl blinked as the flickering lights in the goggles went out. Breaking from the trance, she looked around and found herself in a chair with her arms and legs bound. When she tried to move, she screamed in pain.

Evelyn pressed a button on an intercom and her voice came through speakers in the room. "I would resist the temptation to stretch," she said, staring at Elastigirl through a glass wall that divided them. "The temperature around you is well below freezing. Try to stretch, and—you'll break."

"So you're the Screenslaver," Elastigirl said, shivering.

"Yes and no," said Evelyn, crossing over to get a closer look at Elastigirl through the glass. "Let's say I created the character, and I own the franchises."

"Does Winston know?" Elastigirl asked.

"That I'm the Screenslaver? Of course not. Can you imagine what Mr. Free Enterprise would do with my hypnosis technology?" she said sarcastically.

"Worse than what you're doing?" said Elastigirl.

"I'm using the technology to destroy people's trust in it. Like I'm using Superheroes."

"Who did I put in jail?" asked Elastigirl.

"Pizza-delivery guy," Evelyn said. "Seemed the right height, build. He gave you a pretty good fight. I should say I gave you a good fight through him."

Elastigirl said Evelyn was smart for hypnotizing someone to play the hypnotizer. "But," she asked, "it doesn't bother you that an innocent man is in jail?"

"Ehh, he was surly. And the pizza was cold," she replied.

"I counted on you," said Elastigirl.

Evelyn smiled. "That's why you failed."

Elastigirl wanted an explanation.

"Why would you count on me?" said Evelyn. "Because I built you a bike? Because my brother knows the words to your theme song? We don't know each other."

"But you can count on me anyway," said Elastigirl.

"I'm supposed to, aren't I? Because you have some strange abilities and a shiny costume, the rest of us are supposed to put our lives into your gloved hands. We're helpless, and Superheroes are the grand answer."

"But why would you— Your brother—"

"—is a child," Evelyn finished. "He remembers a time when we had parents and Superheroes. So, like a child, Winston conflates the two. Mommy and Daddy went away BECAUSE Supers went away. Our sweet parents were fools to put their lives in anybody else's hands. Superheroes keep us weak."

"Are you going to kill me?' asked Elastigirl.

"Nah," said Evelyn. "Using you is better. You're going to help me make Supers illegal forever." She pressed a button, igniting the lights on the goggles, and Elastigirl's eyes glazed over as she fell back under Evelyn's wicked spell.

18

Out in the Parr backyard, Violet and Dash watched as Bob brought out Jack-Jack wearing his new suit.

"Ready . . . laser eyes!" said Bob, demonstrating.

Jack-Jack appeared to concentrate, and rays came out of his eyes. They landed on a target wrapped around a patio umbrella, and the umbrella snapped in half.

"Stop!" said Bob. Jack-Jack stopped.

"Wow!" said Dash.

"That's not all—watch this," said Bob. "Jack-Jack . . . blaster. Ready?" Bob picked up Jack-Jack and held him with his belly down. Then he said, *"Pew! Pew! Pew!"* Giggling, Jack-Jack fired lasers as Bob aimed.

"Whoa!" said Dash. "No way!'

"That is CRAZY COOL!" said Violet. "Let me try him! I want him!"

"I'm just demonstrating. No firing the baby around the house, you understand?" said Bob, chuckling. "We're trying to teach him to control his powers."

Jack-Jack squealed in excitement, loving every second of the special attention. The tracker sounded an alert, and Bob picked it up. It read MORPH IMMINENT.

"See the screen?' said Bob, showing Dash and Violet.

Jack-Jack let out a playful squeal and disappeared into a blue vortex.

Bob pointed to the screen. "That's the current readout," he said.

Violet held the tracker and swept it around until it beeped. Dash and Bob followed her as she moved into the house with the tracker, trying to find Jack-Jack.

"Click it!" said Bob. "See the readout? Dimension 3. See the shape? That's the room. See where he is in relation? So where is he?"

Dash looked over Violet's shoulder as she panned the device across the family room, finally landing in the corner.

"He's THERE!" Dash exclaimed, pointing. He held out a cookie and Jack-Jack appeared, gobbling it down. Everyone cheered!

Suddenly, the Incrediphone rang, and Bob rushed to pick it up. "Elastigirl is in trouble," said Evelyn.

"What happened to her?" asked Bob.

Evelyn said she didn't want to tell him over the phone. "Meet me on our ship at DevTech," she told him.

"The ship at DevTech. I'll be there in fifteen minutes," Bob replied, and hung up the phone.

"What's at the ship at DevTech?" asked Violet.

Bob didn't answer her. He immediately called Lucius. He asked him to come watch the kids and added, "Suit up. It might get weird."

"I'll be there ASAP," said Lucius. "Fifteen tops."

Lucius hung up and pointed a remote control at the wall. It hissed as it opened, revealing his mounted Frozone Supersuit.

"Where you going ASAP?" shouted Honey from the other room. "You better be back ASAP! And leaving that suit!"

Bob hurried through the family room wearing his Supersuit. "I gotta go," he said to the kids. He told them Lucius would be there soon, and headed out the door.

"WHAT'S AT THE SHIP AT DEVTECH? AND WHY ARE YOU IN YOUR SUPERSUIT?" shouted

Violet. But Bob was already in his car, ripping down the road toward the pier.

Dash headed straight to his parents' bedroom and found the Incredibile remote in the nightstand drawer. He quickly hid it behind his back when Violet burst into the room. She blew right by him and went over to the dresser, pulling open the bottom drawer.

"What's going on?" Dash asked nonchalantly, still hiding the remote behind his back.

"I dunno," answered Violet. "But Dad called Lucius AFTER getting a call about Mom. Then left in his Supersuit." Violet pulled everyone's Supersuits out of the drawer and tossed Dash's to him.

"I thought you renounced Superheroes," said Dash.

"Yeah. Well, I renounce my renunciation. Put that on," she said.

Dash didn't need to be asked twice. He zipped into the bathroom with his suit, and in the blink of an eye appeared again, standing in front of Violet with it on.

The doorbell rang, and Dash rushed downstairs to open it. Voyd, Brick, Reflux, He-lectrix, Screech, and Krushauer stood there, wearing glowing goggles. They were all being controlled by Evelyn.

"You kids aren't safe," said Voyd. "The Deavors sent us—"

Voyd looked over her shoulder, noticing that . . . it was suddenly snowing.

"Well, isn't that redundant!" said Frozone. Voyd and the other Supers turned to see Frozone calmly crossing the driveway. "The Deavors just sent ME here to guard the house." He protectively moved between the kids and the other Supers. "Because the kids aren't safe."

Dash, still clutching the Incredibile remote behind his back, slowly found the button to summon the car.

"I get it—managerial screw-up," said Frozone. "Tell Winston I handled it. You understand, Miss—"

"Voyd," she replied.

"Miss Voyd. Drive safely." Frozone moved to close the door, but Brick stopped the door with her foot.

Dash pressed the summoning button on the remote, and inside Victor Cachet's mansion the Incredibile powered up and took off, blasting a hole through a wall!

"The thing is," said Voyd, "he wants us to bring you, too."

Frozone cracked a smile and started to speak, then—*WHOOM!*—he knocked Voyd back with a wall of snow. He covered it with a blast of ice before slamming the front door. He turned to the kids. "That isn't gonna hold them long. Where's the baby? Dash, grab the baby!"

Dash ran up to get Jack-Jack from his crib as a shower of ice hit the front windows. In a flash, the hypnotized Supers were inside the house, battling the kids and Frozone!

Dash carried Jack-Jack as he tried to run outside, but kept finding himself back in the house. He finally realized he was running through Voyd's portals.

As Frozone tried to fight off Screech, Violet created a force field around herself and her brothers to protect them from He-lectrix's electrical blasts. Then, just as Krushauer began to crush Violet's force field, the Incredibile ripped through the house, stopping right in front of Dash.

"Incredibile! WINDOWS DOWN!" shouted Frozone, the ice-powered hero, as he tried to keep the hypnotized Supers away from the kids. The car windows opened and Frozone turned to the kids and ordered them to dive in. Once the kids were secure in the car, Frozone commanded, "Incredibile! Set voice identification! Loudly—say your names!"

"Violet Parr!" said Violet.

"Dashiell Robert Parr!"

Dash and Violet watched in horror as the hypnotized

Supers restrained Frozone long enough for Screech to put hypno-goggles over his eyes!

"Oh, no—LUCIUS!" said Dash.

Frozone stopped struggling as his eyes glowed. Then he lunged toward the kids.

"NO!" screamed Dash.

"Incredibile! ESCAPE!" shouted Violet.

Just before Frozone could reach them, the Incredibile took off!

19

Mr. Incredible ran onto the hydroliner and quickly found Evelyn.

"Good news and bad news," she said as she led him toward the ballroom. "We've found her, she seems physically fine, but she's had an encounter with the Screenslaver and she's acting kind of strange. In here—" She opened the doors and Mr. Incredible went in.

"Strange how?" he asked. He looked up to see Elastigirl crouched between the wall and ceiling, but before he even noticed her glowing eyes, her fists were in his face. She punched him four times before he could react.

After he blocked the fifth punch, he said, "Helen?" But she was already gone—stretching in a blur behind him. When he turned back, he saw two spinning kicks coming at his jaw. His head snapped back with the force. He ducked to miss the next one and lunged for her, but she flipped him and punched him twice more.

Mr. Incredible and Elastigirl battled it out. Evelyn watched from the doorway, enjoying watching Elastigirl's agility and speed pitted against Mr. Incredible's strength and size. But there was another difference. Elastigirl was using all her skills against him, while Mr. Incredible clearly didn't feel right battling his wife. Finally, when he managed to get his hands on her and keep her still for a moment, he whispered, "Helen . . . it's me!"

Elastigirl kissed him. Thrown off guard, he kissed back. At that moment, Elastigirl stretched an arm across the room and grabbed a pair of hypno-goggles from Evelyn. She slapped them over Mr. Incredible's eyes. He screamed for only a moment, then fell silent . . . hypnotized.

Winston stood on the deck of the hydroliner, waiting for Mr. Incredible, Elastigirl, and Frozone. He had expected them for the big signing ceremony, but they hadn't arrived. Evelyn walked up to the deck, and he asked if she had heard from them.

"They're all on board. They're resting," she said.

"Weird that I missed them," Winston replied. "Well, good. Let's shove off!"

The Incredibile sped away from the Parr house like lightning, taking the kids on a wild ride. Violet ordered it to pull over so they could figure out what they were doing.

Violet and Dash thought about what their father always said to do when facing challenges: analyze their strengths.

"Okay. Bad guys are after us. No Mom, no Dad, no Lucius. But we have our powers. This car. And . . . what?" said Dash, thinking out loud.

In the backseat, Jack-Jack transformed rapidly through his many forms before going back to his normal self. Dash and Violet look at each other, confident that they could take on any problem.

"Incredibile, take us to DevTech," said Violet.

The car shot off toward the pier. But as soon as they arrived, the ship pulled away from the dock!

"I wish the Incredibile could follow that boat," said

Dash, disappointed. The car suddenly backed up—and drove up onto the dock!

"What did you do?" asked Violet.

"I dunno," said Dash.

"WHAT DID YOU DO?" repeated Violet.

"I DIDN'T DO ANYTHING!" said Dash.

The Incredibile launched off the edge of the dock! The kids screamed as it jetted along the water after the ship. The car quickly caught up and pulled up alongside it.

Violet wondered how they were going to get onto the boat.

"Hey," said Dash, "what if the Incredibile has ejector seats?"

The car responded with a message flashing across the dashboard: EJECTOR SEATS ACTIVATED.

"Wait, what? No—" said Violet.

"Yeah, baby!" said Dash, preparing for the ride.

"NO! Don't say any more—" urged Violet.

"MAX POWER!" said Dash.

The message changed to read EJECTOR SEATS: MAXIMUM POWER. Violet tried to get Dash to stop, but he refused to listen. He ordered the car to launch the seats, and the kids shot into the air!

Violet created a force field around them, and they

safely landed on the deck of the ship. Then they started searching for their parents.

Winston Deavor stood at the front of the hydroliner, welcoming the guests as they arrived. "You're in for a treat! This ship is the largest hydrofoil on the planet, so hold on to something, because we're going to open her up!"

At that moment, the hydroliner began to accelerate as its gigantic hydrofoils emerged from the hull and lifted the entire ship above the ocean's surface.

Violet, Dash, and Jack-Jack had managed to slip down to a quiet corridor below the deck. Violet whispered to Dash, "We need to find Mom and Dad. Stay here; I'm gonna search for them." She vanished.

Dash whispered, "Wait—who's gonna watch Jack-Jack?"

Violet reappeared from the shoulders up. "Suck it up. I won't be long," she said. Then she vanished again.

"But—"

"It's up to *us*, understand?" said Violet. "Keep him amused but quiet."

She disappeared, and the door opened and closed as she headed off. Dash scowled. He turned to Jack-Jack, sarcastically repeating his sister's commands, which made Jack-Jack laugh loudly. Dash slapped a hand over his brother's mouth to quiet him.

Violet moved through the ship until she spotted her parents and Frozone heading into the conference room. She hurried back to her brothers and discovered that Jack-Jack was gone! Dash didn't have any excuses, and there was no time to argue. They started using the tracker to search for him.

The delegates and their Supers gathered around a meeting table in the hydroliner's massive conference room. Oversized windows gave a spectacular view both above and below the waterline. The delegates all sat with their respective Supers behind them. Elastigirl, Frozone, and Mr. Incredible entered wearing hypno-goggles. Winston noticed and whispered into the microphone on his lapel, "Hey, did you make them new masks?"

Evelyn sat in the master control room—a transformed security center where she had placed several monitors to provide multiple views of the meeting. She answered Winston by speaking into her microphone, explaining that the masks had night vision and other capabilities. Then she cued him—it was go time. "Aaand . . . we're live in three, two, one . . . go," said Evelyn. They were broadcasting the event across the globe.

"This is a momentous occasion," Winston began. "We've all managed to accomplish something rare in today's world: we agree on something!" The crowd chuckled and cheered before he continued. "We agree to undo a bad decision, to make sure a few extraordinarily gifted members of the world's many countries are treated fairly. To invite them, once again, to use their gifts to benefit the world." He went on to thank everyone and made a special point to thank the ambassador who had been one of the first to express support for the Supers. She shook Winston's hand and then signed the accord.

Violet and Dash were not having any luck finding Jack-Jack, but when they saw his image moving upward on the tracker that Edna had given Bob, Violet gasped. "He's in an elevator!"

"Let's go!" said Dash, disappearing in a blur.

Violet turned to follow Dash when Voyd approached. The hypnotized Super cornered Violet, and they began to battle. Violet threw force fields at her, but Voyd managed to deflect them all by opening portals!

As Dash reached the elevator where Jack-Jack was, he realized Violet wasn't behind him. He darted back and speed-punched Voyd just as she was about to put hypno-goggles on his sister. In a flash, Dash grabbed Violet and took off, escaping before Voyd even knew what happened!

Suddenly, Dash and Violet heard the growling of monster Jack-Jack.

"That way!" said Dash, pointing down a hall. They soon found Jack-Jack, who had transformed into his fireball state. He had set off the sprinklers.

"MAMA! MAMA!" cried a blazing Jack-Jack.

Violet looked down at the tracker, frustrated. "I know he's on fire—just put him out!" she said, punching buttons. Lavender foam oozed out of Jack-Jack's Supersuit, quickly extinguishing the flames. He giggled as he licked up the sweet retardant.

"They're coming!" Violet said, spotting the hypnotized Supers. She grabbed Jack-Jack and they climbed up into the ceiling vent to hide.

Jack-Jack played with the tracker. "Is it okay to give him that?" whispered Dash.

"I wasn't hearing any better ideas," said Violet. She was just happy it was keeping Jack-Jack happy and relatively quiet.

But the hypnotized Supers heard them, and Krushauer used his crushing power to smash and squeeze the metal vent from a distance. The kids were trapped inside!

Violet tried her best to quiet Jack-Jack, but he began to whine and cry.

"I've got you now!" yelled Krushauer, aiming for the exact spot in the vent where they were hiding. Before he made his move, Jack-Jack transformed into a giant baby, bursting through the vent! He knocked Krushauer out—and destroyed the baby tracker!

Violet and Dash had to get giant Jack-Jack to follow them to the conference room. "Cookie Num-Num," Violet said, attempting to coax him with a treat. The massive baby took the cookie, then crashed through a wall and kept going!

Violet and Dash chased him as he ran out of sight, yelling, "MOM-MOM-MOM-MOM-MOM!"

Soon they came to a wall with a hole in it that was the size of a regular baby. It was too small for them to crawl through. Dash peeked his head in and saw Jack-Jack, now back to his normal size, toddling down a hallway.

"I see him," said Dash. "He's getting away!"

"Stand back," said Violet. She created a force field within the hole and began expanding it until the hole had grown big enough for them to fit through. They hurried in to see Jack-Jack penetrating another wall!

"Darn it!" said Dash.

"He's heading for Mom!" said Violet.

They separated and went in different directions, searching for another way to catch him.

In the conference room, Winston announced, "It is done! The world is Super again!" Everyone applauded as people all over the world watched on their television screens, cheering. Winston had everyone pose for a group photo. "Historic occasion!" he said. "Everyone smile!"

The group faced the camera and smiled just as the giant monitors in the room lit up with hypnotic light patterns. Every person was instantly locked into Evelyn's trance.

Evelyn pressed a button, and a monitor in the center of the room switched over to a shot of Elastigirl, Mr. Incredible, and Frozone. The hypnotized Supers picked up the microphone and began to speak. Evelyn controlled their every word.

"Years of mandated hiding and silence have made us bitter!" said Elastigirl.

"Your promises are empty!" said Mr. Incredible.

"We no longer serve you! We serve only us! May the fittest survive!" said Frozone.

They reached for the camera. Everyone watching the live broadcast saw static on their screens . . . and then the signal went dead.

20

Chad Brentley shifted uncomfortably in his chair at the TV studio as he tried to cover for the interrupted broadcast. "Well, uh . . . some very alarming moments there before the, uh, technical difficulties. Please bear with us."

Evelyn watched from her control room as Mr. Incredible, Frozone, and Elastigirl exited the conference room and locked the delegates and their hypnotized Supers inside. They robotically marched to the top deck and toward the command center, quickly disarming the officers on guard. When one of the officers went for his radio, Evelyn ordered the Supers to hold off and let him use it.

"Superheroes have forcibly taken the bridge!" the officer said into his radio.

Then Evelyn commanded, "Now." Mr. Incredible flung the officer into a wall and ripped out the radio equipment. Elastigirl grabbed the steering wheel, directing the ship to head straight for the city. Mr. Incredible crushed the steering wheel, locking it into its current trajectory. The ship was going to crash!

Violet and Dash caught up with Jack-Jack just as he barged into the ship's bridge. Elastigirl, Mr. Incredible, and Frozone didn't think twice when they saw the kids—they instantly attacked! Violet quickly threw a force field around them, deflecting the blows. The three hypnotized Supers stared curiously at the kids through the transparent force field for a moment, almost as if they recognized them. Just then, Jack-Jack penetrated the force field and slowly floated toward Elastigirl!

"What the—?" said Evelyn, watching from the control room, "No, no, no! Put him down!" she ordered.

Elastigirl looked confused as Jack-Jack landed in her arms, upside down. She turned the baby right-side up. Jack-Jack gazed at Elastigirl and frowned at the glowing hypno-goggles. Then he yanked them right off! She blinked as she came out of her trance and smiled at Jack-Jack.

Furious, Evelyn punched at Frozone's and Mr.

Incredible's controls. "GRAB HER!" she ordered.

Mr. Incredible and Frozone lunged for Elastigirl, but she handed Jack-Jack off to Violet and ripped off their hypno-goggles, freeing them from Evelyn's spell!

Evelyn screamed with rage from the control room, "NOOOOO!"

Mr. Incredible and Frozone took a moment to get their bearings. When Mr. Incredible saw Elastigirl, he faced her defensively.

"Hey!" she said. "It's me!"

"Yeah, that's what I thought last time," he said.

Elastigirl quickly tried to explain everything, and told the kids she was very proud of them.

Then Violet tossed her mother's original Supersuit to her.

In the master control room, Evelyn turned on her monitors and activated the remaining hypnotized Supers, commanding them to spring into action. "Phase three!" she announced.

Moments later, the hypnotized Supers burst through the wall, taking Mr. Incredible and Frozone by surprise.

Jack-Jack transformed into a raging monster.

Elastigirl was shocked. "What the— Jack-Jack has powers?" she exclaimed.

"We know!" yelled Mr. Incredible. "Fight now, talk later!"

Mr. Incredible battled Brick as Voyd threw portal after portal at Elastigirl. Elastigirl managed to punch her arm through them and remove Voyd's hypno-goggles!

He-lectrix tried to electrocute Violet, but she protected herself inside a force field. Monster Jack-Jack lunged at He-lectrix and removed his goggles.

Evelyn watched everything unfold from the control room. She was becoming more frustrated by the minute as she lost control of the Supers one by one.

Then Reflux faced Violet and began to spew molten lava toward her. She threw up a force field and blocked it. Frozone blasted the lava with ice, putting out some of the flames. Suddenly, Screech swooped down and grabbed Dash. Thinking fast, Violet picked up Jack-Jack and aimed him at Screech. "Jack-Jack? Laser eyes! *Pew-pew-pew!*"

Screech fell to the deck of the ship and Dash speed-kicked him.

All the hypno-goggles were finally off and the Supers stopped fighting. However, danger was still imminent, as the ship was getting closer to the city.

Then Elastigirl looked up and saw that the roof of

the hydroliner was turning into a jet! "Evelyn! She's escaping!" she exclaimed.

"Go after her. Finish your mission," replied Mr. Incredible.

"I can't just go! What about the kids? Jack-Jack? Who's gonna—"

"Mom!" Violet cut her off. "Go. We've got this."

Elastigirl smiled, gave Violet a nod, and then told Voyd to come with her.

"I'll shut down the engine!" said Mr. Incredible.

"I'll try to slow the ship from the bow!" said Frozone.

As he approached the engine room, Mr. Incredible was confronted by Krushauer, who still had his goggles on. The hypnotized Super compacted a wall around Mr. Incredible. But the Superhero was too quick. He leaped out of the way and threw a large piece of debris at Krushauer, knocking off his goggles.

Krushauer was finally free from his trance, but now rubble was blocking the hallway. Mr. Incredible couldn't get to the engine room.

"You did this. Can you undo it?" Mr. Incredible asked Krushauer.

"No," the Super replied. "To uncrush is silly. Why uncrush?"

"To get into the engine roo— Oh, forget it. We

don't have enough time," said Mr. Incredible as he raced off.

Meanwhile, Evelyn grabbed Winston and dragged him toward her secret jet. He slowly came out of hypnosis and was confused.

"Where are the delegates and the Supers?" he asked.

"Still hypnotized," replied Evelyn.

Winston started to freak out. "Oh, no, no, no—you're the Screenslaver!" he cried.

Evelyn pressed a launch button, releasing the jet from the hydroliner. "Strap in NOW!" she yelled.

Winston glared at her, then shoved her out of his way as he went for the stairs. Evelyn leaped to the controls and hit the thruster. The jet rose from the deck of the hydroliner as she yelled, "IT'S FOR YOUR OWN GOOD!"

"NO!" Deavor yelled back. He opened the door to the jet. "THIS IS!" He jumped out and landed hard on the deck of the ship. Evelyn let out a frustrated groan, then hit a button, sealing the door of the jet.

Winston headed back to the conference room and quickly turned off the hypnosis screen. As the diplomats and their international Supers snapped out of Evelyn's spell, he called to everyone, "We need to get to the back of the ship! All Supers, protect your ambassadors!"

They followed his lead, rushing to the rear of the ship, bracing for the crash.

Elastigirl and Voyd sprinted up the stairs to the top of the hydroliner just in time to see Evelyn's jet lift off into the sky.

21

"Get me up to the jet!" screamed Elastigirl.

Voyd opened a portal, and Elastigirl jumped in, exiting it in the middle of the sky! With nothing to hold on to, Elastigirl began to spiral downward. But then Voyd opened another portal that Elastigirl slipped through. This time, she exited the other end on top of the jet. The winds were so powerful that they sent Elastigirl flying off, so Voyd continued opening portals, catching her until she finally climbed out of one right beneath the jet. Elastigirl stretched her body, reaching inside the portal, and shot herself into the belly of the jet.

When Elastigirl opened the floor hatch, Evelyn saw WARNING flash on her control panel. She immediately knew who it was.

"Welcome aboard, Elastigirl," she said as she flew the jet wildly, throwing Elastigirl around. Evelyn sent the jet straight up and then straight down, spinning and diving all over the place. "Although we haven't reached our cruising altitude, feel free to roam about the cabin."

Elastigirl pulled herself toward the controls and finally reached Evelyn. She went to deliver a punch, but Evelyn quickly placed an oxygen mask over her own face. As she forced the jet directly up into the clouds, climbing higher and higher into the sky, Elastigirl became weaker and weaker.

Down below, the hydroliner was close to crashing into the city.

"I can't get to the engine room!" said Mr. Incredible.

"We gotta do something, because trying to slow it down isn't working," said Frozone.

"Hey, what about turning the ship?" asked Dash.

Both Mr. Incredible and Frozone reminded him that the steering had been destroyed.

"Dash means from the outside!" exclaimed Violet. "If we break off one of the foils and turn the rudder, we can veer the ship away from the city."

Frozone and Mr. Incredible agreed that it was their only option. "I'll turn the front; you turn the rear," said Frozone. He began to freeze the water to knock off the front right foil.

"Using the rudder?" asked Mr. Incredible. "But that's underwater! How am I supposed to get— All right. C'mon, kids!"

As Mr. Incredible and Dash headed belowdecks, Violet stopped them. "Dad! I know this is going to work, but if it doesn't and we crash, my shields are probably better protection than the boat. I should stay here with Jack-Jack."

Mr. Incredible smiled at Violet. "That's my girl."

"Remember, Bob, we're both turning right!" yelled Frozone.

Mr. Incredible found the ship's anchor, broke it off, and strapped himself to the massive chain. He looked at Dash and pointed at the anchor's controls. "Once I turn the ship, you hit the pull-up button."

"Okay, Dad!" said Dash.

He told Dash to lower him slowly, but Dash quickly pressed the button and Mr. Incredible yelped as he immediately plunged into the water. He struggled to dodge the boat's propellers while trying to push the rudder.

After several minutes went by, Violet grew concerned.

"Dad's been underwater too long!" she said. "We gotta pull him up!"

"Wait—it's too soon!" said Frozone.

"Just press the button, Dash!" said Violet.

"Not yet!" said Dash.

Violet looked over the side of the boat and saw that it was starting to turn. It was working! "Dash, now!" she said.

Dash pushed the button, pulling Mr. Incredible up.

Meanwhile, in Evelyn's jet, Elastigirl was struggling to stay coherent, disoriented by the lack of oxygen. Evelyn kicked Elastigirl in the face, sending her flying backward. When Elastigirl landed, she spotted a flare gun that had fallen in the chaos of the fight. She picked it up and fired it at Evelyn's oxygen tank. The force of the impact sent Evelyn crashing through the windshield of the cockpit. She began to plummet toward the ocean! Elastigirl set the jet on autopilot and shot herself out the broken window toward Evelyn. She quickly caught up to her in midair, grabbed her, and expanded into a parachute.

But Evelyn refused to be saved by a Super. She kicked Elastigirl to free herself and continued her descent toward the ocean. Elastigirl again propelled herself toward Evelyn and wrapped her arms around her. Without a second to spare, Voyd opened a portal on the water's surface. Elastigirl and Evelyn fell through the portal and landed safely on the deck of the ship.

Frozone continued to create icebergs in the water until the hydrofoil finally collapsed. As the ship turned away from the city, a giant wave formed. Frozone used his powers to transform the wave into a snowbank, which acted as a soft barrier for the ship to run into. At last, the hydroliner came to a stop in front of a large building. The Incredibles and Frozone had saved everyone!

Elastigirl turned to her family. "I missed Jack-Jack's first power?" she said.

"Actually, you missed the first seventeen," replied Mr. Incredible.

Right on cue, Jack-Jack multiplied himself, and the whole family burst out laughing.

22

Evelyn Deavor was handcuffed and escorted into a police car. She turned to Elastigirl before getting carted off. "The fact that you saved me doesn't make you right."

"But it does make you alive," said Elastigirl.

"And I'm grateful for that," said Winston.

Mr. Incredible walked over to Violet. He had something on his mind. He cleared his throat. "I've been thinking. Tony forgetting you isn't the worst thing. Just . . . take control. Reintroduce yourself. Go up to him and say, 'You don't know me, but I'm Violet Parr.' That'll be enough."

Violet thanked him and gave him a hug.

The Incredibile pulled up, and Dash handed his dad the remote.

Over the next few days, life took a turn for the better. Inside a courtroom, a judge ruled to restore the legal status of the Supers. Elastigirl, Mr. Incredible, and Frozone were in the crowd, cheering and applauding.

In Western View Junior High School one afternoon, Tony Rydinger sat reading. Violet walked up and tapped his book with her pencil. "You don't know me, do you?" she asked.

"No, I don't. . . . Wait," he said, chuckling. "Are you the girl with the water?"

"Violet Parr!" she said quickly.

Tony smiled and shook her hand. "I'm Tony."

The two continued chatting as they got to know each other . . . again.

Early one evening, Tony closed his front door and trotted out to the station wagon waiting at the curb. Violet sat in the back along with the rest of the Parr family. Tony got in and sat beside her.

Violet introduced everyone, then said, "I tried to limit it to *one* parent."

"We're all going to a movie, too," said Helen. "Tony, don't mind us."

"We'll be sitting on the other side of the theater. Not watching you," Bob said. He winked at Tony in the rearview mirror.

"He's kidding," said Violet. "They're only dropping us off at the theater. They have other things to do."

"So . . . you guys are close, I guess," said Tony.

"We can get closer!" said Bob.

"Bob!" said Helen, laughing.

But when they pulled up to the theater, sirens blared as police cars raced past in pursuit of a suspect. The Parrs exchanged glances, and Violet ushered Tony out of the car.

"Here," she said, handing him some money. "Large popcorn, small soda. Save me a seat, center, about eight rows back." Violet hopped back into the car and stuck her head out the window. "Oh, and butter only halfway up, unless you like it all the way through!"

Tony watched as the car drove off, wondering what had just happened.

The Parrs put on their masks, and the station wagon transformed around them into a family-sized Incredi-Wagon. Bob hit the booster and they blasted off after the bad guys—and into a new adventure.

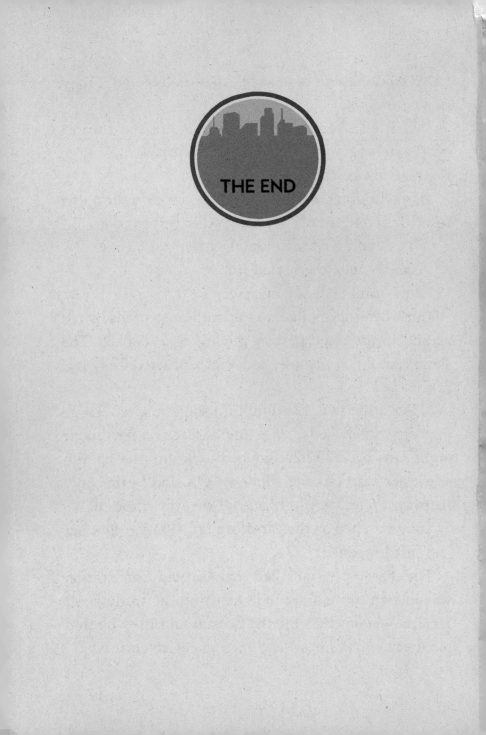
THE END